N

D1715749

MURDER
at the
ACADEMY
AWARDS

MURDER
at the
ACADEMY
AWARDS

a novel by JOE HYAMS

St. Martin's Press : New York

Design by Patrick Vitacco

Library of Congress Cataloging in Publication Data

Hyams, Joe.
    Murder at the academy awards.

    I. Title.
PS3558.Y33M87   1983   813'.54   83-2886
ISBN 0-312-55284-X

First Edition
10 9 8 7 6 5 4 3 2 1

To loyal friends
Bob Phillips
and
Bette Phillips

ACKNOWLEDGMENTS

Most books are the result of
collaborative efforts. This book, in
particular, required the input of
many experts in their fields. I am
particularly indebted to: Detective
J.D. Smith and Sergeant Virginia
Pickering of the Los Angeles Police
Department; Dr. Robert Danbacher,
chief forensic expert, Office of the
Medical Examiner, Los Angeles
County; Barry Fisher, director, Los
Angeles County Crime Laboratory;
Criminal Investigator Dan Ryan,
Maricopa County Attorney's Office,
Phoenix, Arizona; ordinance expert
William E. Rose, Phoenix, Arizona;
computer expert Mat Beck; film
composer and conductor Jack Elliot;
television director Marty Pasetta.
And most especially, my thanks to
film director Elliot Silverstein who
gave unstintingly of his time and
advice and, with editorial consultant
Victoria Pasternack, helped shape a
notion into a book.

MURDER
at the
ACADEMY
AWARDS

PROLOGUE

"THERE'S LITTLE DOUBT IN MY mind that these ballots were marked by the same hand."

Louis Meyer gestured to the portable microscope he had set up on Sadler's desk. "You can see for yourselves. Everyone has a distinctive way of writing, even when making an 'X'. The pressure of the instrument on the paper is similar in most of these ballots. The size and shape of the X is consistent. You can see that in most instances even the same writing instrument was used, because the flow of ink to the point is unique in every pen."

None of the three men standing in front of the small desk took up his offer to look through the microscope. Instead they looked at each other.

The graphologist shrugged and began to pack the microscope into its padded wooden box. He cleared the desktop of his other equipment, then looked at Sadler. "Do you want a written statement from me?"

Sadler, nervously clasping and unclasping his hands, cleared his throat and spoke in a hoarse voice. "Louis, I know what I'm about to say is totally unnecessary between us. But for the benefit of these gentlemen who don't know you as well as I do, I want to request, in their presence, that you keep what you've seen here and the results of your examination completely confidential. May I have your word on this?"

The graphologist offered his hand to Sadler. "You have my word on it, Evan." He walked to the doorway, then turned around. "Gentlemen, today is Sunday and I have spent the entire day with my family. There will be no bill, no record of this visit or of my having seen or met any of you. Good day."

The group of men sat mute until they heard the sound of the front door closing. Will Thomas turned toward Sadler looking haggard and ashen, as if he were personally responsible for his employer's difficulties. In a sense he was, since it was he who had reported the discrepancies.

"Well, how do we handle the announcement?" Sadler asked.

"What announcement?" asked a fourth man who had sat silently in the corner of the den during the graphologist's report. He had been introduced by Martin Wood as a senior vice-president in charge of programming at the network, an executive with the power to make the final decision about the fate of the show.

"That we're canceling the show tomorrow, naturally," Sadler said.

"No, we're not." The executive stared into Sadler's eyes, which flickered briefly to Martin Wood, who looked away.

"We *must*," said Sadler. "Our integrity has been compromised. We have hard evidence that someone has tampered with the ballots."

"Evidence? What evidence?" the executive asked.

"You heard what Louis said."

"I'm sorry, I don't know whom you're talking about."

"The graphologist!" Sadler was getting angry.

"I don't know anything about any graphologist. All I know is that my network has presold a two-hour prime-time show to several national sponsors, and cancellation of that show will cost the network two hundred million dollars, to say nothing of causing a two-hour gap in our prime-time scheduling. Now I have a question for you, Mr. Sadler. Are you and your firm prepared to cover those losses incurred by your failure to perform a service for which you contracted?"

Sadler's heart began to thump in his chest. "My reputation is at stake here, and I will not compromise my firm's integ—"

"What the hell has integrity to do with it? You are supposed to be accountants, not private investigators." He lowered his voice conspiratorially. "Your friend Meyer said there was 'little doubt' in his mind. Which means he had *some* doubt. If this were a court of law, I could find as many experts to dispute his findings as to corroborate them. I, for one, am not going to piss two hundred million dollars down the drain on the word of a man who has doubts. Are you?"

Sadler shifted his weight uneasily, glancing again at his old friend Wood. "Speaking for the Academy, Martin, what's your position?"

"We're in a bind, Evan," Wood said. "The ballots are in, the promotion has been started, and the program scheduled. I tend to agree with your friend here. We don't have enough evidence to cancel the show, and if we did, the publicity would be disastrous to us all."

"Gentlemen, gentlemen, don't look so glum," the network executive said. "This isn't the end of the world. We merely go ahead as scheduled and everything will be all right. I promise you."

Wood fidgeted in his chair, and for a few moments no one spoke. Sadler looked out the living room window toward the ocean. In the distance he made out a group of surfers congregated like gulls. His own boyhood had been spent solemnly with books and studies, and he envied the young surfers their freedom from responsibility.

Sadler was the first to speak. "A few irregular ballots could mean the difference in a close vote." His voice was low and full of anguish.

Another pause.

"Couldn't we discard the bad ballots?" Wood asked hopefully.

"Not until I find out how they came into our possession," Sadler said.

"Maybe it was a mechanical error," Wood offered.

"No, it wasn't," Sadler's voice rose sharply. "What do you think I've been doing since Will first told me about the irregularity? I personally called the printer who has done our work for thirty-five years. He assured me it was impossible for any numbers to be double printed. Will and I then checked all the other possibilities for mechanical failure. There simply aren't any."

Wood reached into his pocket for cigarettes. "Do you mind?" he asked.

Sadler did mind. He forbade even his wife to smoke in the living room because the fumes clung to the draperies. But he nodded assent.

Wood blew out the match and took a long drag. "I gave up smoking four months ago, but this morning . . . Had I known what you were considering, I'd have brought a bottle of Maalox instead."

Sadler coughed from the acrid smoke. "As I see it," he said, "we have no option other than to admit publicly that our integrity has been violated in some way."

The network executive interrupted. "You both sound like politicians. We're not talking about national security here. We're talking about an entertainment spectacular that will lose us millions of dollars in revenue if it's cancelled."

"Need I remind you of Watergate?" Sadler asked heatedly. "It all began when a guard discovered a door taped open. With just one lie, the entire government and the president of the United States were toppled."

The network executive pounced on him. "And need I remind you that if you cancel this show, the public—and the press—will wonder how often in the past your firm's integrity has been breached? Awards for every year in history will be suspect."

"That's a risk I'm willing to take," Sadler said.

"But it's not a risk *we're* prepared to take, at least not on the basis of such flimsy evidence."

"What do you suggest we do?" Sadler asked Wood.

"We're in this together," Wood said, "and we must—we will—stick together. What I suggest is that you continue tabulating votes, continue your investigation. If, and I underline *if*, you find any hard evidence of further irregularities, contact me at once and we will proceed from there. Until that time, we should all forget ever having had this conversation."

Wood looked at his watch. "And now that we have the matter resolved, Evan, I'm going home. My wife is having guests for brunch, and I don't want to be late."

"Resolved" was hardly how Sadler saw the matter. He feared he would be hearing from Wood and the network executive again, and soon.

CHAPTER *1*

MATT SHAW SLIPPED OUT OF bed quietly and pulled on a pair of swim trunks. He padded lightly down the stairs and out into the cool morning air. The beach at Malibu was deserted except for a few gulls probing masses of kelp washed ashore by the tide. The damp sand crunched under his naked feet.

He stood at the water's edge and breathed deeply, then plunged into the light surf. He sliced easily through the water, his strong arms carving out powerful strokes. Once beyond the breaking waves, he rolled onto his back and floated, looking up at the wisps of clouds trailing across a clear sky.

Something brushed against his leg. His body tensed, then relaxed as he reached out to catch Eva's wrist. She gulped a mouthful of air and dove below the surface. His hands tugged at her bikini bottoms, trying to urge them down over her hips.

She struggled to the surface, feet scissoring to tread water, and pressed her breasts against him, one hand slipping down inside the front of his trunks.

He stiffened against her fingers, encircled her warm

7

body in his arms, and closed his mouth on hers. Despite the cold water, heat rushed into his loins as he sank below the surface. Pushing away from his embrace, she let her lips graze his chest and then his thigh. For a moment he held her shoulders, but she wriggled free, only to come up a moment later behind him, one hand sculpting the contours of his swim trunks.

"Race you back," she said, her low sensual voice vibrating in his ears. She turned toward shore. He swam after her but she stayed a length ahead. Suddenly she caught a wave and body-surfed to the beach. She was laughing when he came out, but Matt's heart was thumping and his face was set with frustration.

"Goddamn it, you've done it to me again," he said.

She hopped up and down on one foot like a child, her head tilted to one side, trying to shake water out of her ears. "What you mean is, I *didn't* do it again. We had a deal, remember? Last night was our farewell performance."

Matt reached for her, but she darted toward the house. He tackled her just before they reached the steps leading up to the wooden sun deck. In a moment she was on the sand beneath him, his knee separating her legs. "No one can see us here," he said. His mouth sought hers and his nostrils filled with the clean salt smell of her body.

Eva struggled against his weight; then suddenly she began pummeling his chest with her fists. "I said no and I meant it," she said between clenched teeth.

"You never said no before."

"Well, I am now. Nobody, but nobody fucks me unless I want it."

Surprised and hurt, he released her. "Hey, what was all that business about in the water?"

"That was fun."

"Well, it turned me on."

"Then turn yourself off. I'm starving and I have one hell of a busy day."

She got up, brushed the sand off her back and bounded up the steps to the house. He watched the motion of her long, slim legs and tight buttocks. She was tall and lean, with short-cropped hair bleached honey-colored from the sun. In a bikini she looked like an athletic teenager. Dressed, she had the cool elegance of a Grace Kelly. That contrast in styles was part of her charm.

The smell of fresh-brewed coffee assailed him when he entered the kitchen. Before going for his swim he had started breakfast. He now poured orange juice into two tall glasses and dropped two English muffins into the toaster. When they popped up, he spread them thinly with diet margarine and grape jelly, and put them on her French country china. From a cabinet, he took down two floral-patterned cups and saucers, poured the coffee and added a spoonful of diet sweetner to his. He emptied the remaining coffee into an insulated carafe and put everything, including white linen napkins, on a breakfast tray.

Balancing the tray carefuly, he climbed the white carpeted stairs to her bedroom and nudged the door open with his foot. Shafts of sunlight came through the picture window overlooking the ocean. Everything in the room was white, and he squinted against the glare.

She was already back in bed, the top sheet drawn over her breasts. "My favorite meal of the whole day," she said as he set the tray on her lap.

"There are meals and there are meals," he said suggestively.

"Get your mind off sex, Matt. I'm running late. And I told you, I've got appointments back to back all day, which is why I'm up so early." She picked up a coffee cup, and he reached for a glass of juice.

He sat down on the bed next to her, his weight causing the mattress to sag. He was tall, four inches over six feet in his bare feet, with the physique of a college gymnast. He was five years her junior. "Every boy should have an older woman teach him about love," she had told him. But to his annoyance, the teacher-pupil relationship had carried over into every aspect of their lives together.

She nibbled at the muffin with her small pointed teeth. "What are you going to do with yourself?"

"I'll get by," he said, trying to sound more assured than he felt. The knot in his stomach had tightened. He wondered how she could eat.

"I'm sure you will, Matt. You've got lots of talent. But I don't want you to get into trouble again."

"After today I'm no concern of yours any longer."

She put down her cup, smiled at him and shook her head. His mother had made the same gesture whenever they discussed what he was going to do with his life. His irritation grew.

She reached out and took his hand. "Don't think I don't appreciate what you've done for me. But we made a business arrangement and I intend to stick with it. You have your part in the film, as I promised. And as for the rest—you and me—that was something wonderful and exciting I hadn't planned on. But it's over now and it's time for us to go our separate ways. We discussed all this. You know how I feel."

She opened the drawer of the nightstand and took out a flat gold cigarette case. It was fitted with an insert that held neat rows of pills for each day of the week. She pried most of the Friday column out with her buffed and polished, natural-colored fingernail. Tossing four vitamin capsules into her mouth, she swallowed them with a few sips of orange juice.

Matt watched her while she finished eating. Then he lifted the tray off the bed and put it on top of the chest of drawers, leaving his plate untouched. "We could renegotiate, Eva." He hated the note of pleading that had crept into his voice. He hadn't wanted to love her. In fact, he didn't actually like her very much. But she excited him as no other woman had.

She looked out at the beach, avoiding his eyes.

"When it's over with you, it's really over, isn't it?" Matt persisted.

"You said it. Now, please get the hell out of here so I can get dressed and go to work. And I'd like you to be out of the house before I come home. I'm having a friend over for dinner."

"Already?" He tried to dull the edge of jealousy in his voice.

"Give me a break, Matt," she said. "It's a female friend. Now fuck off."

Downstairs in the kitchen, he went about the business of cleaning up, trying to quell his anger and hurt.

Soon he heard her on the front stairs. He looked out the door and saw her in the hallway, dressed in a tight-fitting simple tan sheath. Her footsteps continued past the kitchen and the front door opened and shut. Her Ferrari's engine filled the silence, then receded down the Pacific Coast Highway. You manipulative bitch, he thought. One day you'll get yours.

Director Robert Goldman settled down in the mobile control room. This was his last run-through of the entire show, cueing more than a dozen of his camera crew on their moves. On the lighted stage, the 100-piece orchestra rehearsed the theme music from the five nominated films, playing just enough bars of the theme to make it recognizable. During the actual ceremony, the amount of time those few bars would be repeated would be determined by how long it took the winning producer to get from his or her seat in the audience to the dais.

The orchestra leader held up one hand, fingers spread wide apart to signify that they were to repeat the theme from the fifth nominated film.

In the dim upper balconies, the cleaning crew put the finishing touches on the auditorium. In the last row of the third balcony, a maintenance man meticulously brushed the seats searching for each speck of litter left from the evening before. Backing down the aisle, he nearly stumbled over a tape recorder in front of a spectator seated in one of the last rows. Its owner quickly picked up the recorder, switched it off, tucked it under his arm and quietly left the building, leaving the maintenance man mildly puzzled as he completed his task.

The black studio limousine inched its way toward the Dorothy Chandler Pavilion in the early evening traffic. On the street, excited fans cheered and shouted as their favorite stars passed by. Inside the limousine which had picked her up at her home in Malibu, Eva Johnson nestled deeper into her borrowed Russian sable, its luxurious feel delighting her. A young girl peered into the car window, turned to a friend on the sidewalk, and announced loudly, "Nobody."

Eva was amused. The girl was right. She *was* nobody. But within three hours, things would be different. They would all know her name. She could visualize the next morning's headlines: YOUNGEST FEMALE PRODUCER EVER TO WIN THE AWARD. She pulled the fur closer around her.

The chauffeur's voice interrupted her thoughts. "The Award telecast is beginning, Miss Johnson. The switch is on your right."

The small color television on the console facing Eva flickered on. She turned the volume low.

"Set working okay?" the chauffeur asked.

"Perfectly," Eva replied.

The TV screen showed an aerial view of the Pavilion. Shafts of white light from carbon arc lamps crisscrossed the sky over the building, giving it a cathedrallike effect. The image on the screen shifted to the line of cars. Hundreds of tiny pairs of lights, resembling a shimmering serpent, approached the Pavilion. Eva leaned forward to study the screen, trying to locate her limousine in the motorcade.

Then she took a small gold compact from her evening bag and flicked a switch, illuminating a makeup mirror in the arch of the roof near her shoulder. She studied her face with objective detachment. Her gray-green eyes had irises striped with a faint horizontal line of tortoise and dark brown. The full mouth wore a thin coat of colorless lip gloss. Honey-colored hair framed an oval face. Only her nose, which tilted slightly at the tip, was imperfect, but it gave sensuality to the face. Lips pursed, she patted a touch of light powder on high cheekbones for emphasis. Satisfied with the effect, she switched off the light and put the compact away.

Hers was now the second car from the carpeted entrance to the Pavilion. "Mr. and Mrs. Michael Caine!" The crowd shrieked with frenzy as a male voice announced the celebrities over the public address system. The British actor, resplendently handsome in a tuxedo, helped his beautiful Eurasian wife from the back seat of a white Rolls-Royce. The Caines disappeared from Eva's sight with a covey of tuxedoed escorts, only to reappear on the TV screen a moment later inside a roped-off corridor where Army Archerd was conducting a series of impromptu interviews.

Eva had an overwhelming sense of déjà vu when her car's TV and the public address system simultaneously announced, "Arriving now is Eva Johnson, producer of *The Reckoning*."

As Eva tentatively put her foot out the door, inexplicable, bone-chilling fear, a dark premonition that she should not get out of the car, kept her from moving. Her mouth was suddenly dry. Her breath came shallowly. "Miss Johnson?" The chauffeur's voice snapped the tension.

She composed herself, took a deep breath, and accepted the chauffeur's hand.

The crowd cheered and applauded as Eva stepped out onto the street. Exhilarated, she lifted her head high and threw back her shoulders. She was five feet eleven inches tall with high heels, and possessed that disturbing and rare combination of unrestrained sexuality with the wholesome, open face one usually associates with Scandinavian travel posters. She smiled, waved, and blew the crowd a kiss, hardly aware of the studio press agent guiding her now by the elbow and whispering, "We've got to hurry or you'll miss Army's broadcast."

A familiar voice called her name. Her eyes searched the crowd. Matt, wearing his old windbreaker and jeans, towered over the spectators near the entrance, smiling at her and giving her a thumbs-up sign for good luck. She met his eyes briefly, then turned away. The press agent urged her forward.

The ceremonies were scheduled to begin in minutes. There was pandemonium outside the Pavilion as uniformed guards and ushers tried to hasten the celebrities inside before the doors closed promptly at 7:30. In her element now, Eva strode across the lobby like a huntress, forcing the press agent into a trot to keep up with her. As she walked, she casually let the sable slip from her broad bare shoulders, exposing the simple, flesh-colored evening gown that had been designed to emphasize her firm, high breasts and narrow waist.

Half a dozen people interrupted her progress to wish her luck, and the rush of adrenalin made Eva feel lightheaded. She nodded briefly to the well-wishers, murmuring appropriate thanks, and continued toward the area where the pre-Award interviews were being telecast live to an estimated three hundred million viewers.

A dark handsome man with an aquiline nose and wavy brown hair etched with gray streaks reached over the rope barrier to pull her into his arms for the traditional Hollywood salute, a kiss on both cheeks. Newsmen moved in to take pictures of David Braverman, head of World Studios, with his current protégé. But only Eva heard his hoarse whisper: "If you do it, you won't live to see tomorrow's headlines."

Eva forced a smile. She was about to tell him not to

worry, that she had changed her mind, but he disappeared into the crowd. Army Archerd took her arm.

"For our last interview tonight," Archerd said, "before the show you've all been waiting for, we have Eva Johnson, producer of *The Reckoning*. Are you excited about your film, Miss Johnson—only your second as a producer—being nominated for Best Picture?"

"Very," said Eva, adding hastily, in accord with long tradition, "but most important to me is the fact that my peers in the film industry saw fit to nominate it for this honor."

"You know," said Archerd, "you're so beautiful, I'll bet some of our viewers wonder why you never wanted to become an actress."

"I did study acting in high school," Eva said mechanically, repeating the story she had so often told during newspaper interviews, "but I was too tall for most of the boys in my class. The only part I ever played was Juno, and I was terrible. Afterwards, my mother insisted I study typing. She told me to learn some trade I could do sitting down."

"What can you tell us about your next film?"

"Only that it will probably be for another studio."

Archerd's eyebrows rose, but there was no time left for him to continue the line of questioning. Behind Eva a stage manager had signaled time up.

"Thank you, Eva Johnson," Archerd said hurriedly, "and good luck tonight."

Seated in the nominees' section of the elegant auditorium, Eva was acutely conscious of the empty seat on her right. The doors were about to close, and Cheryl had promised that, for once, she would be on time.

Eva glanced around her. She was surrounded on all sides by more than two thousand of the most famous people in show business. Cary Grant, still outrageously handsome, was seated directly in front of her with his bride of less than a year. Al Pacino, sporting a bushy beard, took his seat down front and caused a stir. Pacino was seated next to Farrah Fawcett, radiantly beautiful in a shimmering gown that revealed an enticing bust. Eva had once tried on one of Farrah's gowns at the studio and marveled that the actress's bosom was smaller than her own.

The Pavilion overflowed with beautiful women wearing exquisite gowns and priceless jewels and furs taken out of the vault only once or twice a year. The men were turned out in the latest French and Italian evening clothes. Everyone wore their best public manners, well aware that the eyes of the world were on them as they paused to throw kisses to friends and wish them luck.

The house lights began to dim, and people hurried to take their seats. Eva noticed heads turning. Someone behind her said, "What's *he* doing here?" She swiveled around and locked eyes with Mickey Levy. The pudgy gangster's face was expressionless, his eyes dark and threatening. Eva flushed and turned away. Levy, escorting his daughter Ginger, continued down the aisle and took a seat just behind Al Pacino. Eva sighed with relief, until Levy turned around and sought her eyes. In the darkness, her hands trembled.

The entire Award ritual was held in accordance with longstanding tradition. Two stars standing behind a spotlit lectern in stage-center alternately read aloud the names of the five nominees for each category. A sealed white envelope was then handed to one of the presenters by the tailcoated representative of Evan Sadler, Inc., the accounting firm that tabulated and certified the accuracy of the votes. A dramatic hush fell over the audience as the envelope was opened, followed by tumultuous applause after the announcement. Theme music from the winner's film was played as he or she dashed or glided to the stage, accompanied by more applause. One of the stars then handed an Award to the winner, who usually delivered a short speech of thanks to everyone associated with the film, plus any friends or family he could think of.

When the technical awards began, Eva joined everyone else in perfunctory applause as each nominee was announced. Ever aware of the cameras, the audience applauded the winners with apparent enthusaism. The acceptance speeches were dull, tedious, and pretentious, but Eva scarcely heard them. She was formulating the words she would use when her own turn came.

By the time the acting awards finally began, Eva was toying with a new notion.

> "It is with deepest feeling that I want to acknowledge those members of the Academy and certain studio executives who tried so hard and for so long and with such commitment to prevent me from standing here at this moment. I wish to speak now to you. I cannot name you individually, but as I look upon you tonight, certain glances and shifting of weight tell us both you know who you are. . . ."

Robert Goldman looked at the quartz clock on the director's console. It was 9:47. Just thirteen minutes and he could collapse and forget for another year the forty-five small monitors spread across the wall of his master control van in the Pavilion parking lot. His head was pounding, and his throat was raw. The cigarettes plus the coffee had taken their toll, and the pressure of trying to compress a three-and-a-half hour show into three hours hadn't helped.

His eyes flicked to the clock again. In twelve minutes it's over—we're home free, he thought, eyes expertly scanning the monitors. "Tighten to a shoulder on that brunette. I don't want the boobs hanging out," he told camera four over his intercom. He knew that although Americans like cleavage, it might be offensive to some viewers in the other sixteen nations receiving the telecast live by satellite. "You're next, and then we go to the stage!"

"Ready, four," said the associate director on Goldman's right. All eyes went to the preview monitor as camera four zoomed in, and the brunette was flashed around the world, minus her offending cleavage.

"Take four," said Goldman.

"Ready six, on the whole house," said the A.D. The technical director punched a button, and camera six's image jumped to the preview monitor.

"Ready three, wide on the stage!"

"Take three."

"Ready two, on the podium."

"Four, show us the house."

"Take two."

"Ready four."

"Take four."

His crew worked together like a military drill team. He thanked God.

The drumming of applause filled the auditorium, its steady beat leading up to the focal point of the evening, presentation of the Award for the Best Picture. Eva's welling excitement had an almost sexual intensity. The rhythm of her life until this moment had been peaks and valleys, positive and negative, each movement bringing her closer to the orgasm which would culminate in ecstasy, fulfillment, and ultimate calm.

The huge auditorium stilled. Camera three was focused wide on the stage where Al Pacino and Jacqueline Bisset were behind the podium preparing to read off the names of the films nominated for Best Picture. "Ready two," Goldman said, eyes on the monitor. "Crane left. Hold it. Take two."

"One, three, five, six and nine, ready on the nominees," said the A.D. The monitor showed the Sadler representative handing a white envelope to Jacqueline Bisset. Five other monitors relayed pictures from the audience of the five producers of the five nominated pictures.

Jacqueline took the envelope. "And the winner is—" Then, not disguising her shock, she said, "*The Reckoning!*"

There were stunned murmurs of disapproval from the crowd.

"Ready nine on Johnson," said the associate director inside the control booth.

"Shit, that's a surprise!" said Goldman.

"And here to accept the Award is the producer, Eva Johnson."

"Take nine," said Goldman. "Ready four on the house."

Eva rose uncertainly. Applause started to build perfunctorily. She took a deep breath and glanced around her.

"Take four, nine hold!"

Suddenly she felt a chill. Nicholas! She had not noticed her ex-husband sitting across the aisle. She shook off the image of his pinched white face and the malice in his expression.

"Take nine, pan her to the stage."

She headed down the aisle. There would be no gushes of surprise or shouts of delight from him. Throwing back her shoulders, she regained her cool, regal bearing. And that was the image she projected as she hastened down the row toward the dais, concerned only with her triumph and new status in the motion picture community. Nothing and no one could spoil this moment for her.

The clapping became more intense as Eva mounted the three carpeted steps to the podium, carrying herself like a royal bride on the way to her prince, refusing to allow herself to be rushed by the impelling beat of the orchestra.

"Take two, carry her to the podium. Four, gimme her ex-husband."

She focused on her timing, calculating her arrival at the podium for the moment the familiar music would reach its brassy peak.

"Take four on Riddle. Two hold."

"Take two."

As she stepped up to the podium, hand outstretched for

the coveted award, Eva doubled over. The muscles of her face contorted. Gasping, she fell to the floor, her body twitching with pain.

Goldman couldn't believe his eyes. Had Eva stumbled or fainted, or was she having a seizure?

"Camera two, stay on her," he barked into his headset.

"What the hell's going on, Eddie?" he asked a stage manager.

"I don't know," came the reply over Goldman's headset. "She just collapsed."

Goldman's thoughts were in conflict. An audience of 300 million people had seen Eva collapse. His first instinct was to cut to a commercial. But the world would want to know what was going on and would resent being cut off from it.

"Camera two, hold on her," he ordered. "Eddie, find Carson. Have him get on stage fast, and talk!"

A tuxedoed man from the audience dashed to the stage, shouting, "I'm a doctor, let me through, please."

The group surrounding Eva gave way. The doctor knelt down and placed a hand behind Eva's neck, the other on top of her head. He lifted her neck and extended her head so the chin pointed straight up.

"Someone telephone the paramedics," he said.

He pinched Eva's nostrils shut with the index finger of his right hand and began mouth-to-mouth resuscitation.

"Is she dead?" someone asked.

The doctor ignored the question.

"Nah, she's probably just stoned or drunk," someone volunteered.

"Camera two, loosen up," Goldman ordered. "Eddie, for God's sake, get Carson on stage and have him reassure everybody that it's going to be all right!"

Johnny Carson, white-faced and nervous, appeared on camera. "Miss Johnson has collapsed," he said to the stunned audience. "We don't know just what the problem is, but there is a doctor in attendance."

The first notice of a medical emergency at Chandler

Pavilion was phoned in by a stagehand to the Hollenbeck Fire Station four miles away. The call was logged in at 2155 hours, and the three-man paramedic unit instantly rolled, siren screaming.

The doctor put the heel of one hand over the lower half of her breastbone, the other hand on top of the first. "Does anyone here know how to do mouth-to-mouth?" he asked as he began rocking forward, using the weight of his upper body to exert pressure on her chest.

"I do," said a woman in the crowd.

"Then do it."

Goldman decided that what was going on might upset children in the viewing audience. "Camera six, stay on Carson. Eddie, get Carson to cue a commercial!"

The stage manager held up a cue card in front of Carson with the word "Commercial."

"We'll be back to you in a moment," Carson said. "In the meantime, we have this message."

"Standby commercial," Goldman said into his headset. "Roll commercial. Take it away."

His instructions were received twenty miles away in the studio master control booth. The master monitor now showed the image of a beautiful woman holding up a can of spray deodorant.

Death does not come instantly, even in violent circumstances. Sometimes life just seems to ebb away as perception disappears. So it was with Eva. She drifted in and out of consciousness, aware only of a slow procession of gradually dimming images, strange faces peering at her, the murmur of voices.

Security guards swiftly and efficiently carried Eva to the rear entrance of the Pavilion. A crowd of newsmen had already gathered.

Matt had seen Eva's collapse on the television screen set up in front of the building and had rushed around to the back, trying to push his way through the guards.

"I'm her boyfriend," he explained frantically. A burly

guard noted his windbreaker and jeans and held him back. Matt shoved at the guard, but was restrained by a carotid hold on his neck. His mouth alongside Matt's ear, the guard growled, "Now beat it, son, before you get hurt." He released Matt and pushed him back into the crowd.

The ambulance screeched to a halt. Two paramedics hurried out of the back of the vehicle carrying a stretcher.

Eva heard her name being called as from a vast distance. Then she felt her body being lifted and carried. But her brain was aware only of the sensation of drifting in a cocoon of warmth down a long, narrow tunnel. She was calm and peaceful now, her struggle over.

"I think we've lost her," said the paramedic who was performing cardiopulmonary resuscitation in the back of the ambulance as it sped, lights flashing and siren screaming, to White Memorial Hospital ten miles away.

When Eva was brought into the Emergency Room, the doctor in charge took only a minute or so to pronounce her dead on arrival. He picked up the phone and dialed the County Medical Examiner's office to file a report.

CHAPTER *2*

A HOMICIDE DETECTIVE IS AN organization man. He goes to his office every morning wearing a suit and tie, and attends meetings and conferences during which he conducts his business. There are procedures to be followed, reports to be dictated, phone calls to be made and returned, people to be interviewed, specialists to be consulted, facts to be researched and verified, and other departments of the organization to be contacted.

The captain of homicide delegates authority because, like any other executive, he cannot devote his full energy to a single matter. There are always calls on his time demanding immediate attention, always other employees' problems to be considered, conflicting schedules to be sorted out, shortages of personnel to be handled, and higher-ups in the organization to be answered to.

A captain of homicide is not like any other executive, however; most executives rarely look death in the face. A homicide detective sees death in all its varied forms at least half a dozen times a week, sometimes more. And he sees it at its worst—gunshot wounds and stab wounds and ice pick wounds, mutilations and eviscerations. And each time he looks at another human body that has been mutilated, he loses a sliver of his own humanity.

So it was with Captain Phillip Roberts, "Punch" to most of the 2,177 employees of the Los Angeles Police Department. He was the quintessential detective. A big man, loose-limbed, strongly built but past the age when the sum of his physical power was greater than his parts, he still moved in a manner that made certain women think about big cats and certain men think carefully before challenging him.

A Marine Corps hero in Korea, Punch had played pro football with the Pittsburgh Steelers. But a knee injury ended his career, and he went to California for a visit. He liked it so much he decided to find a job, and joined the police department where his ascent through the ranks was spectacular. Because he preferred his fists to his nightstick, he was soon dubbed Punch, and the nickname stuck.

Just now, on this Tuesday morning in April, he was adding to his reputation on the pistol range by putting nine of ten .38-caliber slugs in the black, thus qualifying for an additional $10 bonus in his $3,083 monthly paycheck.

In the stall to his right, Detective Sergeant Bonny Cutler was also qualifying. The range master's voice over the loudspeaker boomed through Officer Cutler's plastic ear protectors. "Ready on the left. Ready on the firing line." A brief pause, and then, "Commence firing."

Bonny dropped into a crouch. Grasping the snub-nosed Colt .38 with both hands, she cocked the hammer back with her right thumb, sighted down the barrel at a target seventeen yards ahead of her and to the right. She took a deep breath and pulled the gun toward her body with her left hand, pushing forward simultaneously with her right. "Squeeze," she said to herself as she exhaled a quarter of her breath and tightened her finger on the trigger. The bullet left the cylinder. The gun bucked up and to the right. Bonny brought it back down until the target appeared again on the tip of her front sight. She repeated the breathing routine, squeezing off each shot as rapidly as possible. She fired her last round just as the range master shouted, "Cease fire."

Bonny's brow was beaded with perspiration and her hands were shaking slightly as she flipped the cylinder catch forward to eject the empty shells, which clattered onto the concrete. After glancing into the cylinder to be certain it was empty, she laid the revolver on the shelf in front of her. Hands still trembling, she turned a large crank to the left of the cubicle and reeled the target back to her station. There were holes scattered around the edge of the black bullseye. She held the target up for Punch to see.

He grinned proudly, squeezed her shoulder and said, "You're getting good, Sprout."

Bonny signed her name and badge number on the bottom of the target and turned it in to the range master. Outside, in the Police Academy parking lot, it was hot and muggy. Punch and Bonny walked in silence to the drab, olive-colored Plymouth sedan which the city provided for its detectives. Punch opened the passenger door for Bonny, one of the few traditional concessions to her gender she permitted, and that only when they were alone.

It had been that way since they first met years earlier when she was a rookie. They had been assigned as a stakeout team in Griffith Park where the Lover's Lane Bandit was operating. Their assignment was to park in an unmarked car near the planetarium and act like lovers. For several nights they held each other in an embrace, she with her arm around his neck, .38 in hand, and he with his .38 behind her back. One night he kissed her tentatively. Before the assignment was over they were lovers.

Before starting the car Punch brought Bonny's hand to his mouth and brushed it lightly with his lips. "We've got time for dim-sum at the Mirawa," he said.

"I'm with you, Captain, you know that," said Bonny, squeezing his hand. "There's nothing I like more than a Chinese breakfast, unless maybe it's you."

Punch shot her a glance. "Then let's roll. I'm starved."

As they drove out of the lot, Punch opened the glove compartment, flicked the radio to the police band and turned the volume to low.

"I heard on the radio this morning that girl at the Awards last night died of a heart attack," Bonny said.

"What was her name again?"

"Eva Johnson," said Bonny. "According to the news she was only thirty-three."

"You know, the odds against a woman that age having a heart attack are staggering. I wouldn't be surprised if there's more to it than that."

Suddenly the police operator's voice burst through the transceiver: "Two-eleven in progress at liquor store, corner Sunset and Spring Streets. All units in area respond. Code two. Repeat, code two."

Punch picked up the microphone on the dash. "Unit seventeen-A two blocks from two-eleven in progress. Now proceeding to the scene."

He looked over at Bonny. "Buckle up, honey," he said automatically.

They raced through the light morning traffic without lights or siren and arrived at the store less than three minutes after receiving the call. Punch skidded to a stop. He and Bonny were out of the car instantly. Punch used his door as a shield. Bonny, still on the passenger side, leveled her gun on the car hood. Two men were backing out of the store in a crouch.

"They're armed," Punch said. "Watch out for bystanders. Police officers!" he shouted. "Drop your weapons!"

Both men whirled around and fired. Punch and Bonny returned their fire simultaneously.

One of the men fell to the ground. Suddenly Punch heard Bonny gasp, "I'm hit."

Punch fired another shot and the second man fell. Then he ran around to Bonny's side of the car. She was lying face up on the ground.

"I'm all right," she said, forcing a smile. "I think it's only a flesh wound from a ricochet."

Two other police cars quickly arrived. Uniformed officers dashed from the cars, guns drawn. They rolled the wounded men over and handcuffed their hands behind their backs as Punch radioed Parker Center, requesting two ambulances. "Make it fast," he said, his concern not for the wounded robbers but for Bonny, who was quietly moaning on the pavement.

A dark stain was slowly forming on the ground under her buttocks. "You're going to be all right, Sprout," he said, and cradled her in his arms while they waited for the ambulance. The first arrived within minutes.

"There's an officer down over here," Punch shouted to the paramedics. They ignored the wounded men and dashed across the street, quickly examined Bonny, then lifted her onto a stretcher. Punch walked alongside, clutching her hand as they bore her to the ambulance. "I'm going to be just fine," she said. "I'll probably even be ready for dinner tonight, though I think I'll have to miss breakfast. How 'bout a rain check?"

"I'm going to the hospital with you," he said, as they loaded the stretcher into the vehicle.

"No, you're not," said Bonny. "You stay and handle the report."

Grim-faced, Punch watched as the robbers, hands still cuffed behind them, were lifted onto stretchers and carried into the second waiting ambulance. One of the men was cursing vociferously. The other was unconscious. "I hope you die, bastard," Punch thought as the ambulance, siren blaring, roared away.

"It's all over, folks," an officer announced to curious bystanders crowding around. "Go on about your business. There's nothing to see."

A Department criminalist and police photographer pulled up, followed by the press. Punch refused a reporter's request to pose for pictures with his gun drawn, and made only one brief statement: "Two suspects were wounded and apprehended during the apparent commission of a robbery at a liquor store in downtown Los Angeles. A police officer was also wounded. The suspects and the wounded officer have been transported to the hospital."

The criminalist, a recent college graduate, was new to the department. Another goddamn greenhorn, Punch thought irritably. But he knew the young man had a job to do, and he reluctantly joined him in a squad car. The criminalist asked a multitude of questions about the incident, recording Punch's responses on a department form. Punch looked at the sandy-haired young man distractedly, noting his horn-rimmed glasses and the bow tie riding just below a protruding Adam's apple.

After repeating a question for the second time, "Bow," as Punch had begun to think of him, asked if he was all right.

"A detective was shot," Punch said. "I'm concerned about her welfare."

"I understand," said Bow, although Punch knew he didn't understand at all.

It was almost an hour before Punch was finished and able to telephone the Emergency Room from a pay phone to check on Bonny's condition. The nurse who answered the telephone told him she was in stable condition.

"Will she be all right?" Punch demanded.

The nurse's voice was firm and professional. "I told you, sir, she's in stable condition."

"When will she be released?"

"We're keeping her overnight for observation," the nurse snapped, and the line went dead.

"I'd like you in my office as soon as possible." The Chief's voice, like the Chief himself, was imperious, even over the intercom.

"I'm on my way," Punch said. He had been in his office only a few minutes and was filling out a report of the incident in triplicate. He put the papers in his drawer and walked quickly down the cream-colored corridor to the Chief's office. He was waved in by a patrolman-receptionist.

Punch knocked twice on the Chief's door. A latch clicked and Punch went inside, shutting the door carefully behind him.

The Chief stood up behind his desk, framed for a moment between the California and American flags on either side of him. A tall man resembling Walter Pidgeon, with a patrician face and full thatch of white hair, the Chief favored English-cut, tight-waisted flannel suits in the office, and wore his uniform only to official events. It was his stately bearing as well as the authority of his position that always made Punch uncomfortable in the Chief's presence, overly conscious of his own stocky figure, his face scarred by too many cleats, fists and forearm shivvers, and a wardrobe bought at year-end sales.

"I've just heard about the shoot-out this morning." The Chief fingered the file on his desk. "I have only one question. How was it that Detective Cutler, who is assigned to Vice and works the night shift, happened to be with you at the time you received the two-eleven?"

Punch fought against the surge of adrenalin and looked straight at the Chief. He was reminded of lion traps he had seen in films; beneath the Chief's question was a pit with a row of spikes which would impale Bonny and him if he slipped.

"It's all in my report, sir," Punch said. "Detective Cutler was on the range qualifying at the same time as I was. We walked out to the parking lot together and stood talking next to my car. Just as I was leaving, the two-eleven came over the radio. I guessed I was probably the nearest unit, and I felt I would need backup, so I ordered Detective Cutler to join me."

"She left her own car in the parking lot, I assume?"

"She did, sir."

"Very well, Captain. Good show all around. I've

checked the hospital. Detective Cutler will be fit for duty within two days. I'll see to it that you both receive commendations in your files."

Punch stood up. "Thank you, sir. Will that be all?"

The Chief smiled thinly. "For the moment, yes."

CHAPTER *3*

R<small>EESE DONOVAN HAD BEEN</small> probed, poked, fingerprinted, photographed and stripped of all his usual bluster and pride. To make matters worse, he now had a cellmate, a balding fat man in a large Hawaiian print sport shirt and baggy polyester slacks riding two inches above his black shoes.

"Ain't I seen you before?" the fat man asked as the cell door clanged shut behind him.

"I don't think so," said Donovan stiffly, sitting face in hands on the bottom bunk.

"Yeah, I *do* know you. You used to be Reese Donovan. I seen your pictures when I was a kid." The fat man shoved his face close to Reese's. "I'm right, ain't I?"

"You're right," said Donovan wearily.

The fat man settled down on the bunk, his weight causing the springs to sag ominously. "What're you in for?" he asked.

Donovan wanted to summon up a mask that would discourage further questioning, but he was too tired. "I beat up somebody," he said.

"You're kidding! There ain't a mark on you! You must a done a good job to end up here."

"I did," said Donovan.

"What'd the guy do to you? Try to mug you?"

"Why don't you leave me alone. I'm worn out."

"Have it your way," said the man defensively. "But this here you're sittin' on is my bunk. You're up there."

Donovan started to protest, thought better of it and climbed into the top bunk. He stretched out, eased his head onto the hard pillow, and put the tips of his fingers under his chin. He tried to control his breathing, but instead of relaxing, he became acutely conscious of the clashing discordant sounds in the concrete and steel cell block of the county jail. He felt the eyes of the fat man on him.

"Name's Leo Abarbanel," he said when he finally got Donovan's attention. "I'm a comic. I work places like the Comedy Store. The cops busted me last night for obscenity. Fifth time in two months. It's a violation of my civil rights is what it is, but my fucking lawyer is out of town for a couple of days, and his asshole partner says he can't get me out of here until tomorrow the earliest. Who'd you beat up on, pal?"

"My wife," muttered Donovan.

"She have it coming?"

"I thought so."

"She running around on you?"

"Just a domestic problem," said Donovan.

"Yeah, well, those things happen. You get a good lawyer, you'll be outta here by midday."

"I hope so," said Donovan.

" 'Less, o' course, they lay a heavy charge on you like attempted manslaughter. Then it could take hours."

"Nothing I can do about it from here," said Donovan bitterly.

"You don't look like the kinda guy that would bust up his old lady for no reason," said Abarbanel.

"I've never hit anyone in my life before this." Donovan rolled over in his bunk and faced the wall.

"I don't cotton to beating up on broads, but sometimes the cunts got it comin'."

"This one did," said Donovan, his voice muffled by the wall.

The gun gleamed in a patch of sunlight streaming onto the polished walnut desk. David Braverman studied it with distaste. Why was it called a "thirty-eight," he wondered. Why not a thirty-five or a thirty-six? He hefted the weapon, which fit his hand perfectly, and aimed it out the window toward a messenger scurrying along the studio street below. How easy it is to take someone's life from a distance, he thought.

Braverman put the gun back into his briefcase, pushed the chair away from the desk and lit a cigar. He paced back and forth in front of a long leather couch, his thoughts uneasy. He had first made love with Eva on that couch. Suddenly he felt old, weary, and unaccountably sad. But this is no time to be maudlin, he thought, shaking himself back to the present. There were matters he needed to attend to. Eva was dead, and he needed to find a way to slip the gun back into the prop department before its absence was noticed.

Mickey Levy climbed the pearl-gray carpeted stairway to his bedroom and undressed, neatly draping his suit and tie on a wooden valet. He then went into his bathroom, the most elaborate money could buy. The walls were mirrored floor to ceiling, the black marble sunken tub had a built-in jacuzzi and gold-plated hardware. The washstand was also of white Carrara marble, and there were ultraviolet lamps on the ceiling so he could get a tan while shaving. One of the mirrored doors opened into a redwood sauna. The other door was a two-way mirror that concealed the shower. He could look out, but no one could see in.

Mickey entered the enormous shower. He had it fitted with a multitude of jets from the walls and ceiling and a Lucite seat so that he could sit by the hour, hot water streaming into his every pore and crevice.

A Beverly Hills psychiatrist, one of the many who had

interviewed him over the decades, had compared Mickey's fetish for washing with Lady Macbeth's. But the psychiatrist was wrong. Mickey had no guilts about anything or anyone, including men he had murdered or had ordered killed. He just liked to sit in the shower. It relaxed him. He imagined problems washing down the gold-plated drain.

And one major problem had just been removed from his life: Eva Johnson was dead. But he still had one piece of unfinished business before their account was squared.

The communications switchboard at Parker Center averages more than five thousand incoming calls every twenty-four hours, and Officer Bob Banner had been on duty for half of his eight-hour shift. Unlike most of the eighteen officers assigned to the emergency switchboard who had requested desk jobs, Banner was doing penance for using undue force during the arrest of a black robbery suspect. He longed to be back on the street where he was working with faces, not merely voices and computers.

An electronic switchboard in the dispatcher's office charted all incoming calls, showing how many were in progress, how many were waiting after getting a recorded message, and how many hung up before a line cleared. Banner glanced at the switchboard and sighed; he still had six calls waiting, and there was no end in sight. During the thirty minutes since his coffee break, Banner had talked to sixteen people. Most of the calls were not emergencies.

Problems ranged from the inane to the urgent. A woman asking how "a friend" could retrieve a purse from a mailbox. "How did she happen to drop the purse into the mailbox?" Banner asked. "She was drunk," the woman replied. A man reporting that three men in a back booth of a Hollywood coffee shop had a gun and the waitress was there alone and scared to death. Banner asked if there was a holdup in progress or if the men were brandishing the gun. "No," the caller said, "the gun's just lying there." Banner filled out a blue card and put it on the conveyor belt in front of him. Moments later, the dispatcher glanced at the card and broadcast a semi-emergency man-with-gun call to all Hollywood units.

Banner's orders were to get the information required and terminate each call as quickly as possible. It was 1450 hours when he flicked to his next call and said mechanically, "Officer Banner speaking. May I help you?"

"I know who the murderer is," said a voice in his headset. Banner decided the caller was a middle-aged black woman. "What murder?" he asked.

"Well, Eva Johnson, of course."

"Yes, ma'am," said Banner. "What information do you have?"

"Well, I know who did it."

"Who, ma'am?" Banner was already convinced he had another crank call on the line. He was well aware, however, that every incoming call was tape-recorded, so if someone later complained an officer was brusque or rude, the complaint could be checked out by listening to the tape. The last thing he needed was to be brought up on charges of being hard on another black.

"I want to talk with a policeman."

"Of course, ma'am, we can send a car out with a policeman if you'll give me your location," Banner said, forcing himself to be patient.

"I don't want a policeman coming here, not to my home!"

"I see," said Banner. "Well, suppose I send a plain-clothes man in an unmarked car?"

"Could he meet me somewhere else?"

"We can arrange that," said Banner. "May I have your name and telephone number?"

"Athena Bigson, B-I-G-S-O-N. I was Miss Eva Johnson's maid."

The name sounded familiar to Banner as he jotted the data on a blue file card. "I'll pass your information on to the concerned detectives, and they will call you and set up a convenient time and place," he said. "What is the phone number where you can be reached?"

Athena gave the telephone number of the house where she would be working later in the day. "When did you say they'll come?" she asked.

"Just as soon as I can contact the investigating officers, ma'am."

Banner looked at the name he had written down. Eva Johnson. Suddenly he remembered where he had heard it. She was the producer who had died during the Academy Awards ceremony. He called his supervisor. "Hey, Sarge, I think I got one here that bears a little attention."

The sergeant played back the tape and scratched his head. "I dunno anything about Homicide investigating an Eva Johnson," he said. "Sounds like a crank call to me."

After her daughter's death, Kirsten had asked Alex Nelson to lock up Eva's Malibu house. Now the stockbroker stood at the open front door, his face registering shock verging on panic. The Eames table in the foyer, one of Eva's proudest possessions, lay shattered on the marble floor. The house was deathly still. As Alex walked tentatively into the house the only sound he heard was his heart pounding.

He looked into the living room. Two white Eames chairs by the entrance were upended. The huge white couch in front of the fireplace was overturned and slashed. Foam, feathers and bits of fabric covered every inch of the room like snowflakes. An eight-by-ten-foot Yael Burke rope weaving that Eva had recently commissioned from the Israeli artist lay in a dismantled heap on the floor.

The foul odor of garbage assailed his nostrils. He made his way cautiously through the living room into the kitchen. All the drawers were turned out. China, cutlery and pans were strewn on the floor amidst slashed boxes of cereal, sugar, rice and crackers. The contents of the refrigerator had been dumped. The door swung open and the light had gone out. The odor came from food rotting in the sunlight.

Nelson turned and ran up the stairs to Eva's bedroom. Breathless, heart pumping, he saw the bedroom curtains had been torn down, the carpet ripped up. Sheets were crumpled on the mattress. Books and scripts from Eva's night table were scattered by the bed. An empty film can lay open amid the rubble on the floor.

He knelt and rifled through the mess until he found what he was looking for. Hands trembling, he opened a hardcover copy of *Scruples* and scanned the flyleaf. On it was a list of numbers written in pencil. He shut his eyes in gratitude, then tore the page out and put it in his pocket.

More relaxed now, he continued surveying the mess. The contents of Eva's closet were stacked high on the floor. Even her bathroom had been ripped apart. The medicine cabinet was open, jars of lotion and pill bottles had been emptied on the tile floor. The lid to the toilet bowl was in the bathtub.

He went back into the bedroom and picked up the white Princess telephone that lay on the bed. He dialed. A woman's voice answered.

"Sweetheart, sit down and listen to me." His voice was hushed and guarded. "The house has been broken into and vandalized, but they didn't get the book." He quickly added, "Don't worry, I'll take care of everything. I'm going to call the police and wait for them here. Then I'll come back to you. Don't panic. Everything is all right. I love you."

He called information next, then dialed the emergency number of the sheriff's station in Malibu and reported the burglary.

Fifteen minutes later a squad car pulled into the driveway. Alex greeted a young policeman at the front door. He carried a clipboard under his arm.

"I'm Miss Johnson's stockbroker," Nelson explained. I came to lock the house up, and when I arrived a few minutes ago, I found this mess." He opened the door wide and followed the policeman inside.

The officer walked slowly through the house, making notes on his pad but not touching anything. On the second-floor landing, he turned to Nelson. "Whoever broke in was obviously looking for something. There's no way of knowing whether they found it or not until we know what's missing. Do you have an inventory of Miss Johnson's valuables?"

"No," said Nelson. "And her mother's in no shape now to handle this."

"You said the owner is dead?"

"Yes, she died Monday night at the Academy Awards."

"When was the last time someone was here?"

"As far as I know, Miss Johnson herself was the last person. She left from here by limousine Monday night to go to the Awards."

"Anyone live here with her?"

"She had a boyfriend," he answered slowly. "I think he sometimes stayed overnight."

"What's his name?" The officer rested the pen on his clipboard.

"Shaw, I think, Matt Shaw."

"You know where he works or lives when he's not here?"

"No."

"He have a key?"

"I doubt it. Eva was a very private person. I don't think she'd give someone a key to her home."

"Not even a boyfriend who sometimes stayed over-night?"

"Her mother was the only other person I know who had a key."

The officer tucked the clipboard under his arm. He left the stockbroker alone in the living room and went to his car to radio in a report.

The county pathologist who performed the autopsy on Eva Johnson reported that there were no entrance or exit wounds, and assigned the death to "perforation of the aorta, cause unknown." A note appended to the report and initialed by the pathologist read, "Bob, I think this is one for you."

Bob Dahlstrom, assistant to the chief medical examiner for Los Angeles County, had started his career as a bottle washer in the county morgue while finishing high school at night. He was thirty-six years old before he earned a degree in forensic pathology. Sometimes he wondered whether it was worth all the work: twelve years of college to become little more than a butcher in an abattoir. Most of the cases were so routine.

He scanned the report of the autopsy conducted that morning on Eva Johnson, age thirty-three, resident of L.A. County, and glanced at his watch. It was 4:45, too late to do a post-mortem himself. He made a note to do it first thing the next day, hoping this one might present a challenge.

"Was it one of my shots that killed the man?" Bonny asked.

"We won't know until the autopsy," said Punch.

They were lying in the king-sized bed he had bought after his divorce, since Bonny had refused to sleep with him in the bed he had shared with his wife.

Bonny was silent for a few moments. "I love you," she said quietly. "I really love you. Do you know that?"

"I know it," said Punch. "Now try to get some sleep. I have pills if you need them."

"All I need is you."

Punch lay still beside her, staring into the dark. Just when he thought she had fallen asleep, Bonny spoke again. "I was afraid."

"So was I," he said. "It's only natural to be afraid when someone is shooting at you."

Bonny had learned that one of the robbers had died when the press descended on her hospital room to take pictures of her. She was hailed in the evening papers as a heroine, the first female officer on the force to be involved in a gun fight.

"But I didn't think about getting shot. I only thought,

that man's trying to kill us, and I fired back. He wasn't a man then, only another target on the range."

"You did exactly the right thing," said Punch.

Bonny got up on one elbow and looked into his face. "Will it always be like this? One minute we're holding hands in the car, and the next minute it's kill or be killed?"

Punch pulled her gently into his arms. "In two years I'll be eligible for retirement. Hang on just a while longer and we'll both quit, buy a van, and travel. Do all the things we've talked about doing."

Bonny disengaged herself from his embrace. "I don't know that I can wait that long, Punch."

He touched her face. Her cheeks were wet with tears. He kissed her gently at first, then passionately.

"Mind my bandaged butt," she whispered, and opened herself to him.

CHAPTER 4

PUNCH DIDN'T MIND THE EARLY morning traffic on the Ventura Freeway leading into downtown Los Angeles. The ninety minutes spent each day commuting from his home in Chatsworth to Parker Center was time he enjoyed. He relished the surge of power when he stepped on the accelerator of the 1967 Porsche he had rebuilt himself, and he liked listening to the stereo turned up at full volume to a music and news station.

He had left Bonny still sleeping, and his thoughts were on her when a car directly behind him honked several times and the driver flashed his lights. Punch was doing the legal fifty-five, so he held his place. The other car roared by on the right. The driver, a teenager, held up one finger in a time-honored salute. For a moment Punch was tempted to undo his badge from his belt and wave it at him. He grinned to himself at the thought of the kid's reaction.

"And as I reported yesterday, the coroner is still attempting to solve the medical mystery of Eva Johnson's death." Rona Barrett's voice came over the radio. "Meanwhile, there's a move afoot to investigate the Award her picture received last Monday night, an award which was obviously not popular with the audience. This tragic affair may develop into the most bizarre scandal to hit the film colony in decades."

If the coroner had reason to believe there was a possibility that Eva Johnson had been murdered, thought Punch, why hadn't his department been notified? It was standard practice for the coroner to keep Homicide informed every step of the way when they were investigating suspicious deaths in the county. Punch knew enough about gossip columnists to sense that Rona probably knew more than she was revealing. He decided to make a brief detour, and swerved onto the San Bernardino Freeway.

The morning newspapers headlined the death of Eva Johnson, but the small man in a pin-striped suit and neat patterned tie sitting alone in a booth of the Pink Turtle, the Beverly Wilshire Hotel coffee shop, was more concerned with the headline in *Daily Variety*, the film industry trade paper: "AWARD SCANDAL BREWING."

Evan Sadler's manicured hands shook as he sipped his coffee, impatiently waiting for his chief accountant, Will Thomas, to join him.

Promptly at 8:45, Thomas appeared, wearing a suit almost identical to Sadler's, but with a regimental striped tie of blue and Harvard crimson. The tall, slim man with the high, domed forehead and the steel-rimmed glasses magnifying his pale blue eyes slipped into the booth beside Sadler. "Did you hear what Rona Barrett said this morning?" he asked.

"I never listen to gossip columnists," Sadler answered.

"She says the police are investigating Eva Johnson's death," Thomas said, as he ordered orange juice and coffee for himself.

"That's to be expected," Sadler said. "We both saw her die, and no one seems to know the cause of death. In any event, Will, it has nothing to do with what I want to talk with you about. I'm planning to open a new branch of the firm in San Francisco."

"You never mentioned that before," Thomas said.

"You know I don't like to talk about things until I have them worked out in some detail. You're the first person in the firm to know, and I'd like to keep it that way for awhile." This seemed to console Thomas. Sadler continued. "As you know, we already have some important clients in San Francisco. They've been after me for years to open an office up there. Last month I looked into the situation. The potential for new business is enormous. With the clients we already have on hand, we can open a small office and show a substantial profit. My intention is to find a location on Montgomery Street, put you in charge, with one or two other accountants under you at the beginning. You can hire secretaries and staff as necessary. What do you think so far?"

Thomas frowned. "It sounds interesting, Evan, but I don't know how Vivian will react. She just finished re-decorating the house, the kids are in school, and she's not going to like the idea of moving and starting all over again."

"I don't know how soon it will be necessary for you to actually move, Will. My notion was for you to spend a month or two in San Francisco with Vivian and get some-one to take care of the kids—at company expense, of course. Scout the potential. When you have sufficient facts and fig-ures, we'll discuss permanence. Meanwhile, I don't have to tell you that your position as partner in the parent firm will remain unchanged. If and when we decide the move is prac-tical, we can talk over terms, and I can promise you I am prepared to be generous."

"Is there any urgency to this, Evan?" Thomas asked uneasily.

"Well, yes and no. A realtor there has found some of-fices which seem to meet our requirements." Evan avoided Will's eyes. "I'd like you at least to look them over. So why don't you plan to spend next week in San Francisco and give me a report. After that, we can discusss the plan at more leisure."

As Sadler had anticipated, Thomas agreed. With him out of Los Angeles for the next week, Sadler would be the only one available to parry any questions that arose concerning the Awards. And, if an investigation began, he would keep Thomas in San Francisco as long as necessary.

Punch drove past the four-level downtown interchange and turned off at State Street, which dead-ended at a complex of county buildings. His badge gained him entrance past the uniformed guard, and he drove directly to the faded, cream-colored Medical Examiner's building. A civilian in the lobby took his name and buzzed Deputy Coroner Bob Dahlstrom. Punch waited on a vinyl and chrome sofa, gently massaging his kneecap. He turned at the sound of footsteps on the linoleum floor.

Dahlstrom approached Punch, hand outstretched, his mournful mouth, made all the sadder by a drooping mustache, arranged into a semblance of a smile. He wore a rumpled safari-style jacket and baggy chino pants supported on his lanky frame by a tooled leather belt with a Western-style buckle.

The smile quickly faded and Dahlstrom was serious. "I was thinking of you only this morning," he said, leading Punch to an elevator. A medical technician entered the elevator with them. They rode in silence to the second floor. Dahlstrom led the way to his small office, where he gestured toward a chair and sat down behind his cluttered desk.

"I just heard on the radio that you're looking into the Eva Johnson case," said Punch. "Why hasn't Homicide been informed?"

"This is a kinky one, Punch," Dahlstrom said. "No one except the people in my department should have known about this, but somehow it was leaked. I wanted to see you face to face instead of talking on the phone or making a written report."

Punch nodded. "All right, I'm here now. What's coming down?"

The coroner rocked back in his chair and clasped his

hands under his chin. "One of my assistants reported the cause of death as a perforation of the aorta and theorized it could have been an aneurysm."

"What's that got to do with Homicide?"

"How many people do you know who've died of a perforated aorta? It doesn't satisfy me. I'm planning to do an autopsy myself later this morning."

"Homicide?"

"Wait till the lab reports are in."

"When will that be?"

"With luck, in a couple of days. Hopefully, before I have to release the body for burial."

"A couple of days isn't soon enough, if I'm going to have to begin an investigation," Punch said.

"I only got the prelim report yesterday," Dahlstrom said. "I told you I was planning to get to you today."

"If this girl was murdered, all hell is going to break loose and you know it," Punch snapped. "I don't want to be following a cold trail."

"I'm on the case personally," Dahlstrom said quietly. "I'll give it priority, and I'll call you the moment I know anything. You got a safe number?"

Punch reached into his wallet, took out a calling card and scribbled two telephone numbers on the back. "One is a direct line. The other is my home," he said. "Call me from a public phone if you don't trust your department."

"Will do," said Dahlstrom. He stood up and shook Punch's hand again.

Outside in the parking lot, the sun was beating down and the smog made Punch's eyes water. Yet as he eased himself behind the wheel of the Porsche he was content. He'd known Dahlstrom a long time, long enough to know that, more than just a physician, he was a crack investigator.

"I've been on the telephone most of the day making funeral arrangements for Friday," Kirsten Johnson started to sob. Alex Nelson patted her hand soothingly. "It was terrible. The coroner wanted permission to do an autopsy. And then Eva's accountant called. He wants to see me tomorrow."

"Of course he does," said Alex. "Eva's will has to be probated and her estate sorted out. It's routine, dear. Nothing to worry about."

"He asked me if I knew anything about her investments."

Alex reached into his coat pocket and handed Kirsten some notes typed on a sheet of paper. "The answer is that when you were going through her desk, you discovered this. I told you yesterday that I found her list of stocks when I went through the rubble in her bedroom. I typed this up myself, adding one more. The accountant will just treat it as one of her investments that went sour, and write it off as a loss."

"But what if he finds out that the signature on the check was a forgery?" Kirsten seemed to deflate, her body getting even smaller, as her voice trailed off.

Alex pressed her hands. "You told me that you destroyed the check when it came through with the bank statement."

"I did," said Kirsten, "but don't banks file photos of all checks?"

"They do, but there's no reason for him to suspect anything."

"It was a hundred thousand dollar check, Alex." Her voice was little more than a whisper.

Alex drew her close and stroked the nape of her neck. "The stock isn't worthless yet. There's still a chance it may regain some of its value. No one will investigate, I promise."

Officer Shel Diller hated homosexuals. He sipped his Orange Julius at the stand on the corner of Argyle and Hollywood Boulevard and watched them parading past him in their skin-tight jeans and tank-top shirts, showing off their muscles—or lack of them. He grunted contemptuously as one of them tried to solicit a passing car. He scorned their sequined dreams of discovery by a porn-film producer, and he considered it appropriate that this section of Hollywood was known in the porn trade as "the meat market."

Shel himself was supposed to blend in. He wore faded old Levis, a tight T-shirt, and a silver Mylar windbreaker with PORSCHE running vertically down the left sleeve. He had a two-day growth of beard and his hair was long and unkempt. He felt grubby. But he was assigned to Vice, and this was all part of the game.

Shel kept an eye on his partner, Jerry, who, clean-cut and muscular in running shorts and tank top, loitered near the street corner. The man behind the counter served up Shel's hamburger to go. He paid with a five, pocketed the change after counting it carefully, and sauntered back toward Selma where he would stand and sip his drink until the tour of duty was over, or, if he was lucky, there was some action.

It wasn't long in coming. Suddenly there was a commotion in the middle of the block. Something was up. Jerry was running toward a cluster of screaming people. Shel dropped his lunch on the sidewalk, removed his wallet from his hip pocket with his left hand, and ran toward the crowd, waving his shield overhead shouting "Police!" The crowd parted like magic before him, closing around him again in a wave. As Shel reached the source of the commotion, a black Pontiac Firebird sped down the street. Jerry shouted, "There's a kid down here. I'll phone for an ambulance," and disappeared into the crowd.

A boy with close-cropped, obviously hennaed red-blond hair was lying at his feet, his right arm twisted at a grotesque angle to his side. The boy's face was covered with blood and vomit, and he was groaning with pain. "Police," Shel shouted again. "Stand back and give him some air." The crowd began to back away.

Shel knelt down and the boy looked up at him through glazed eyes. "What happened?" Shel asked.

"He stumbled and fell, asshole," lisped a voice from the crowd.

"Get me an ambulance," the boy on the ground moaned.

"After you tell me what happened," said Shel, taking his notepad and pencil from his jacket pocket.

"Two guys . . ." The boy was having difficulty talking.

"You know them?" asked Shel.

"No."

"Any reason why they beat you up?"

"No."

"Did you hustle them?"

"I'm no hustler," the boy gasped. "I'm an actor."

"No kidding," said Shel. "You ever acted in anything I might have seen?"

"Ambulance," the boy groaned.

"About your acting career," said Shel. "Who've you worked for recently?"

"Johnson, Eva Johnson. She just won an Award. Please, get me an ambulance!"

Shel put his face close to the boy's, so close he nearly gagged from the smell of vomit. "Look, kid, you could be dead before the ambulance gets here. Who're the guys who did this to you?"

The boy rolled his eyes upward. "Ginger," he said.

Shel heard the siren of an approaching ambulance. "Help's coming, kid," he said. "Now, what has Ginger got to do with this?"

There was no answer. The boy was dead.

Officer Diller went to the patrolman's locker room in Parker Center, shaved, showered, and put on clean clothes. Feeling fresh and determined, he went upstairs and presented himself in Punch's outer office. He showed his badge to the policewoman/secretary. "I need to talk to Captain Roberts on urgent business," he said.

"There are channels for you to take and you know it," snapped the policewoman.

Be charming, thought Shel. You've gone this far. Don't blow it with an argument now. "It's personal," he said.

The policewoman looked at him for a long moment, then flicked on the intercom. "Officer Diller from the Hollywood Division says he wants to see you personally, sir."

Punch was annoyed. Any policeman who went over the heads of his direct superiors was open for censure. This Diller, whoever he was, was taking a chance of getting his ass in a sling. There better be a good reason for it. "Send him in."

Punch stared out his window at the New Otani Hotel across the mall, then swiveled slowly around and glanced at the man standing in front of his desk. "All right, Diller," he said quietly. "Let's hear it, and it better be good."

"I was on the fruit detail in Hollywood today, sir, when at fifteen-fifteen hours a male homosexual was assaulted on the street by two male Caucasians who fled the scene in an automobile. The victim was badly and professionally beaten. He was DOA at County. Before the ambulance arrived, I questioned the victim. He told me he was an actor. He last worked for Eva Johnson, the producer who died at the Awards Monday night."

Punch's eyes narrowed. "Go on."

"I asked him who wanted him hurt. He said, 'Ginger.' "

Punch was puzzled. "So?"

"Before I was working fruits, I worked porn for three months. I happened to do some research on Mickey Levy's family. He has a daughter named Ginger. Word on the street is that she's a wild kid."

"So?" Punch asked.

"Like I said, the kid was worked over by professionals. They probably didn't want him dead. Just hurt bad. A friend of the victim wanted to ride with him in the ambulance, but I held onto him for questioning. He confirmed the victim's statement—that he had worked for Eva Johnson. In a porn film."

Punch grinned slightly. He'd seen officers like Diller before. Ambitious and smart, always looking for a chance to move ahead. He'd started as a street cop himself. Now he needed to find out just how smart Diller was. "If all this is in your report, I'd have seen it sooner or later. What's the urgency?"

"It's not in my report, sir. Just the bare facts."

Punch relaxed. Diller was good. "And you figured I ought to know the full story personally. Right?"

"You know how channels are, sir. The connection between Johnson, the victim, and Levy might not have reached you."

Punch's voice was stern. "I don't normally approve of an officer skipping channels, but in this case I think your judgment was sound." He softened his tone. "Now, is there anything I can do for you?"

"Nothing, sir," said Diller. "But if my information is useful, you might keep me in mind if there's an opening in Homicide downtown."

"I'll do that," said Punch, standing up. "Leave your card with my secretary and I'll be in touch."

Diller did an about-face and walked toward the door. "One more thing, officer," said Punch. "Since you omitted some facts from your report, I'd appreciate it if you'd forget them entirely. Unless you hear personally from me."

"Yes sir," said Diller, who closed the door firmly as he left.

In the far corner of the dimly lit bar, a small combo made up in noise what it lacked in quality as Elliott Gruzinsky watched a brunette make her way through the heavy smoke and around the crowded tables. She stopped beside him.

"May I sit down?" she asked.

He looked into his drink.

"Whatever it is, it could always be worse," she said.

"Wanna bet?" he asked, mildly slurring the words.

The brunette sat down carefully. Elliott had noticed her before, watching her leave with men and come back later alone. The black sheath dress emphasized her heavy breasts, which probably attracted most of her customers.

"I'll have a scotch with water," she said to a passing waiter.

Elliott was already feeling better now that he had company. "What's your name?" he asked.

"Louise."

"Tell me, Louise, what's a nice girl like you doing in a place like this?"

She smiled at him. "Just passing through. And what do I call you?"

"Elliott."

"What do you do when you're not getting drunk, Elliott?"

"I'm a screenwriter." Elliott paused and added bitterly, "Strike that. I *was* a screenwriter."

"You written anything I might have seen?"

"I don't know your taste. Maybe you like cartoons or foreign movies."

"Try me."

"It's a long story."

"I'm all ears."

"Okay. You know the movie *The Reckoning* that won an Award Monday night?"

"Is that the one produced by the woman who dropped dead onstage?"

"Yeah, and it couldn't have happened to a nicer person."

"You didn't like her?"

"You might say that." Elliott took a heavy gulp from his glass. "She was a monster."

"Oh?" Louise's eyes were round with curiosity. "What did she do to you?"

"She ripped me off," Elliott said testily. He finished his drink and looked around for the waiter, who was busy elsewhere. "Waiters," he said, "like cops. They're never around when you need 'em."

"You were telling me how you got ripped off." Louise moved her chair closer to Elliott's, her leg touching his.

"Yeah, well, I had an idea for a film, and I took it to a friend of mine. Correction. I *thought* she was a friend. I wrote the first picture she produced, with her fag husband directing. I'd spent months researching the idea for this next one and preparing an outline. Then I took it to her. She read it and said she'd be in touch. Okay. I didn't hear from her again. Weeks later, I read she was producing *The Reckoning.*"

The waiter came over, and Elliott ordered two more scotches and water.

"What did you do then?" Louise asked.

"I called her office but she was always 'in conference.' Finally I got her at home. She admitted the story was mine and offered me minimum scale for it. I hung up on her and called my lawyer. He asked me if I'd registered my outline with the Writers Guild. I hadn't. I figured she'd give me some input and I'd develop it more, then register it. I'd worked with her before and like an idiot, I trusted her."

Louise nodded sympathetically. "And then?"

"Then I called her back and told her if she didn't give me credit and pay me what the idea was worth, I'd wring her neck with my bare hands."

"What did she say to that?"

"She laughed and said she was disappointed in me, that she'd expect a more dramatic means of disposing of her. And she was right. If I were going to do her in, it would be with style. I have a certain fondness for the exotic."

Elliott finished his drink, acutely aware of Louise's leg pressing against his. He felt a tightening in his groin, a pounding at his temples. He stared at her a moment. She was pretty and stacked, in fact, better looking than most of the starlets around town.

"I've got the time and the money if you've got the place," he said finally.

Louise hesitated, then stood and made her way back

around the tables to the door. Elliott followed unsteadily.

"She's hooked another one," said the bartender as he set a beer in front of a regular customer. He leaned forward confidentially. "I'd like to see the look on that john's face when he shows her his cock and she shows him her badge."

There was a line of waiting diners extending onto Ninth Street in front of The Original Pantry when Matt drove by a few minutes before midnight. He parked in the lot across the street, then took his place at the end of the queue. The customers were mainly night workers: taxi drivers, watchmen, city employees, and press operators from the *Los Angeles Times* who had just put the early morning edition to bed.

The restaurant, open twenty-four hours a day continuously for fifty-six years, was an anachronism in an era of modern furniture, subdued lighting and sterile decor. Bare bulbs in the ceilings illuminated tables of rough-hewn oak and straight-backed solid chairs. The dishware was heavy white porcelain from the thirties, as were the chunky coffee cups.

Matt liked it. It was the old Hollywood of the gangster movies. He could imagine Dashiell Hammett or Raymond Chandler eating next to him at one of the family-style tables. It was the kind of place they wrote about, an atmosphere in which Philip Marlowe or Sam Spade would have felt right at home.

As the line shuffled slowly toward the entrance, a white-coated waiter bustled through the door calling out, "Any singles? There's room at the counter."

"I'm single," called Matt, holding up his hand. He shoved his way through the crowd and pushed toward the counter. He was about to sit down when he heard his name. A young man at a long crowded table, a worn leather jacket hanging loosely on his emaciated frame, signaled for him to come over.

Bud Millett had been one of the production assistants

on *The Reckoning*. Matt had noticed him on the set when he stopped by to pick up Eva at the end of a day's shooting. Bud had been friendlier than the other crew members, who seemed to tolerate Matt only because he was Eva's boy-friend. Bud seemed to go out of his way to be cordial.

One evening Matt had asked Eva what Bud's job was. They were having dinner at The Gallery in Santa Monica. Eva considered her wineglass.

"He's kind of a gofer," she said. "He does the kinds of things you can't ask anyone else to do."

"Deadwood in the budget?"

"Maybe," Eva said, "but it doesn't matter. I owe him. A lot of people in Hollywood owe him, so he gets work."

"What do you owe him?"

Eva looked directly into Matt's eyes. "I'm sorry. I don't think that's any of your business."

Matt walked over to the table and sat down next to Bud, who shoved a large plate of radishes and celery stalks in front of him. "Eat up, pal," he said. "The salad's on the house."

Matt stopped the waiter and ordered a New York steak with home fries, a slice of apple pie and coffee with sweet-ener.

"Sorry about your old lady," Bud said after the waiter left. "Bad karma. Baaaad karma."

"She'd called us off just before the Awards," said Matt, "but I still feel pretty miserable. She'd been good to me. And as far as I knew, she always seemed to be in perfect health."

"Yeah, well, she was like all those other Hollywood bitch-queens. They throw people away like old gloves when they've served their purpose."

Anger rose in Matt's throat. "Just what do you mean by that?" he asked. He noticed that the dark circles around Bud's deep-set eyes seemed to have grown even darker since the end of the film.

"Just a manner of speaking." Bud's tone was conciliatory.

"She gave you a job," Matt said.

Bud turned and looked directly into his face. "I served my purpose," he said slowly.

"And what was that?"

"We can talk about it some time, if you want, but not here."

It was just after 2:00 A.M. at Parker Center when Louise finished her arrest reports for the evening shift. Bonny, just back at work from her hospital stay, looked over at her.

"How'd it go tonight?" she asked.

"About par for the course." Louise's voice was weary. "God, how I hate this lousy job."

"The mayor wants midtown cleaned up of pimps and johns. It won't be long before the heat's off and we're reassigned. Anyway, it's better than juveniles or kid-porn."

"I suppose, but sometimes I feel sorry for the johns. The last guy I busted tonight was nice, the kinda guy I might've liked under other circumstances."

"You can't let them get to you," Bonny said.

"I busted him all right, but I still think he was a nice guy. Said he was a screenwriter. You know that producer who died at the Awards the other night? According to him, she stole his idea for the movie that won. Instead of wringing her neck he went out on a drunk. He was just miserable, looking for a shoulder to cry on."

"He well known?"

Louise shook her head. "I never heard of him but then I don't go to movies much. His name was Gruzinsky, Elliott Gruzinsky."

"I never heard of him, either," said Bonny, "but he should be thankful he's only up for soliciting, not murder. First offense. He'll be on the street in the morning."

CHAPTER 5

PUNCH REACHED TO TURN OFF the bedside alarm. Then he realized it was the telephone. He fumbled for the receiver.

"Is that you, Punch?" Bob Dahlstrom sounded unusually nervous.

"What's up, Bob?"

"You remember that case we were talking about a couple of days ago?"

"Sure do."

"Could you meet me for breakfast in an hour at the Biltmore coffee shop?"

"I'll be there," Punch said.

Bonny sat up in bed. "Anything the matter?" she asked.

Punch leaned over and kissed her on the forehead. "Dahlstrom wants to see me at the Biltmore at nine. You go back to sleep."

"If you cuddle me, I can."

Punch folded her in his arms. He waited a few minutes until he heard her gentle breathing, then got out of bed.

Punch slipped into a booth beside the deputy coroner at the hotel coffee shop.

"The shit's going to hit the fan," Dahlstrom said.

"Tell me about it," said Punch.

Dahlstrom took a quick sip from his mug. "It's been a long night. I had just finished the P.M. on Eva Johnson when I called you."

Punch stirred a heaping spoonful of sugar into his cup. Dahlstrom took a scrap of paper from one of the many pockets of his rumpled safari jacket and glanced at it.

"The decedent was, to all intents and purposes, in excellent physical condition. The cause of death *was* a perforation of the aorta, and that ain't necessarily natural."

Punch sighed. So she was murdered, he thought, and felt sadness for still another victim cut off in the prime of life. Murder was an ugly business, and he hated murderers with a passion—which, perhaps, was why he was so good at his job.

"How was the aorta perforated?" Punch asked.

"Don't know."

"With what?"

"I don't know."

"When was it perforated?"

"Seconds before she died."

"Why do you think the shit's going to hit the fan?"

"The press learned we've been conducting extensive tests on the body. Don't ask me how they found out, but I got a call from the *L.A. Times* just as I was leaving last night, which is why I stayed after hours. I have to release the body for the funeral tomorrow, and I'm going to have to make some kind of statement today."

Punch noticed Dahlstrom's hand was trembling.

"What are you going to say?"

"The usual guarded statement: 'The cause of death is still being investigated and further toxicological and scientific studies are still in progress.' But the press will put two and two together and come up with the right answer."

After his meeting with the coroner, Punch went directly to his office at Parker Center. He reached into the desk drawer and took out a pad of 8½-by-11-inch printed forms. The heading read: Table of Contents for Homicide Case Folder. He tore off a sheet and wrote Eva Johnson's name on top, then began to fill in the information he had at hand.

His telephone buzzed. The Chief's voice said "Roberts" in his typically peremptory manner.

"Yes, sir."

"Have you seen the late edition of the *Times?*"

"Not yet, sir."

"I'll save you the trouble. The headline reads, 'Award Murder Probe.' How come I wasn't told about this—or should I rely on the newspapers in the future for departmental information?"

"There was nothing official until half an hour ago, sir, when the deputy coroner advised me he had reason to suspect Eva Johnson's death was not by natural causes."

"How *was* it caused?"

"He doesn't know yet, sir. He sent the vital tissues in for fluroscopy this morning. He should have a report tonight, but he's certain she was murdered."

"And what is your department doing, Captain Roberts?"

"I'm going to start a full scale investigation today."

"Fine," said the Chief, "but before you do, I want to see you in my office with a full report on what you know and how you plan to proceed. By the way, who's in charge of the investigation?"

"I'll handle it personally, sir."

"Good. Now, how soon can I expect you in my office?"

"Within half an hour, sir."

The line went dead. Punch looked over his duty roster. He was short two men on sick leave; three other detectives were on vacation, the others all had full case loads.

Twenty minutes later he tucked Eva Johnson's case folder under his arm and started down the corridor to the Chief's office. A crowd of reporters and TV cameramen were clustered in the hallway. When they saw Punch, strobe lights exploded in his face and microphones appeared in front of him like stop signs.

"Any suspects?"

"No comment."

"Why do you think she was murdered?"

"No comment."

"How was she murdered?"

"No comment." His voice was rising with irritation.

"Does her murder have anything to do with her winning an Award?"

"No comment at this time!" Punch pushed his way into the Chief's office.

His boss was waiting for him, elegantly dressed as usual. Punch wished he had worn his blue suit this morning rather than his baggy brown slacks, pink sport shirt, and pale blue golf jacket.

The Chief got right down to business. "What kind of surveillance do you have planned for the Johnson funeral tomorrow morning?"

"I'll have two photographers from Intelligence covering the mourners. One of them will mix with the newsmen, and the other with the TV crew. We'll have photos of everyone in the area. And I'll have two detectives among the mourners. I'll also arrange for any men I can spare to be inside the chapel during the services."

"Fine," said the Chief. "Any theories?"

"None yet. First I'll check out the people with motive and access. At this moment, the list is slim, but I'll keep you informed on a daily basis."

The Chief nodded approval.

"How many men can you assign to the investigation full time?"

"As you know, sir, I'm short-handed. My division was recently cut from forty-two detectives to thirty."

The Police Commission had recently ordered the cutbacks as part of what they had described in a news confer-

ence as "budgetary setbacks." Most of the LAPD felt the
Chief had not worked strongly enough to keep the force at
full manpower. Punch's implicit jibe did not pass unnoticed.

"I'll see to it you have all the detectives you need," the
Chief said, finally sitting down and resting his elbows on
the desk blotter, fingers making a pyramid supporting his
chin. He studied Punch thoughtfully for a moment. "Sit
down, Captain," he said.

Punch sank into one of the large red leather straight-
back chairs arranged in front of the desk.

"I don't need to tell you how important it is that we try
to resolve this case as quickly and effectively as possible.
The murder of this young woman was seen on television by
more than three hundred million people around the world.
Unfortunately for all of us, this murder could not have happened at a worse time. Not only is the governor campaign-
ing for reelection, but the mayoral race is also coming up.
Although I have yet to hear from either of these gentlemen,
I assure you I will, and when the pressure comes down on
me, I will in turn put pressure on you and your division. If
we look bad, you will look worse. Do you follow me?"

Punch nodded.

"You are particularly vulnerable to pressure, Captain.
You are eligible for fifty percent retirement in less than
two years. Should this case be resolved to everyone's satisfaction, I will see to it you receive a commendation. On the
other hand, if it drags on, I would not be surprised to see
you in charge of communications until your retirement. Do
I make myself clear?"

"I'm an experienced detective, not a miracle worker,
sir. And I don't like being threatened."

"I'm not threatening, Captain. I'm promising you. I
want to show the world and our critics that the LAPD is on
top of this case. One of the best ways to demonstrate this is
to begin booking suspects. I feel certain that within a few
days your investigation will produce some suspects."

"I'll do my best, sir."

The newsmen scattered like opposing linemen when Punch reappeared outside the Chief's office, the homicide folder tucked under his arm like a football. He bulled his way through the group and stormed into his own office.

The morning shift of detectives stood clustered around the office coffee machine, but when they saw Punch, face flushed and eyes black, they all hastened to their assigned desks. Typewriters suddenly began to clatter.

Punch unlocked a file drawer and took out a small green metal box filled with three-by-five-inch cards arranged alphabetically. This was his personal computer system, programmed almost daily with the names of people he met, their affiliations, occupations, avocations and unusual areas of expertise. He sorted through the cards and began making notes.

Most homicide investigations follow an established routine. When he began a new case, Punch normally moved it through the thirty efficient detectives under his command. But in this instance he was certain the Johnson murder would not be solved by the usual methods. His task here was to try piece together a giant jigsaw puzzle—unrelated bits and pieces of information about the victim which might point to the murderer. The picture would be revealed only when all the pieces fit neatly into place.

A detective in the old tradition, Punch relied heavily on contacts and informants. Like a Mafioso who works on the "you-owe-me-one" principle, Punch had a long list of contacts, informants and friends.

His first call that morning was to Parker Center Communications. Waiting for an answer, the telephone receiver tucked between shoulder and chin, he reached into his drawer and took out a packet of antacid pills and popped one into his mouth. Like many organization men, Punch had ulcers, which, like large bills, invariably presented themselves at the most inopportune times.

Sergeant Lee Siegel was an old friend, and Punch got straight to the point. "What time did you first get a call from the Pavilion about the death of that producer?" he asked.

There was a brief pause as Siegel went through the Monday log.

"The call came in to us at twenty-one-fifty-two and was relayed to Central at twenty-one-fifty-three."

"Did any of our men respond to the call?"

"Negative. It was strictly a medical emergency. Hey, why's Homicide interested? I thought she died of a heart attack."

"The coroner disagrees, so it's in my ballpark now. I'm just starting the investigation."

"Wait a minute, wait a minute," said Siegel. "In that case, maybe I've got something here that might interest you. Hold on."

Punch popped another antacid into his mouth.

Siegel was back on the line almost instantly. "Officer Banner got a call yesterday. I thought it was a crank so I tabled it, but I have the card in front of me. A female informant who claims she was Eva Johnson's maid says she knows who murdered her employer."

"Name?"

"Athena Bigson. She gave two phone numbers where she could be reached during the day."

Punch copied down the name and numbers. "Why didn't you buck this on up to me at once?"

"Anytime someone prominent dies we get calls like this, Punch, you know that. We didn't know anything about the woman being murdered."

"Okay, Lee, but keep me in mind if anything else with Johnson's name comes across your desk."

"Will do," said Siegel.

Punch made several other calls without scoring a hit, then scanned his notes. On a hunch he called the Santa Monica Sheriff's Office, which also covered Malibu, and asked for the watch commander.

A man's voice came on the line and Punch identified

himself. "I understand that Eva Johnson, the woman who died at the Awards Monday night, lived in Malibu. You ever have any reports or business with her?"

"She was one of the more beautiful women on the beach," the watch commander said. "Only time we had any official contact with her, though, was the day after the Awards. A reported burglary. Hold on and I'll get the file."

Punch used his free hand to open the drawer. He reached in to take out another antacid pill, but the package was empty.

"Yeah, I was right." The watch commander's voice had come back on the line. "On Wednesday, we had a call from an Alex Nelson, who identified himself as Eva Johnson's stockbroker, reporting a burglary. A deputy responded to the call. He found the house had been broken into recently. From the way it had been turned upside down, the deputy says he figures it was professionals looking for something special—probably jewelry or narcotics. According to Nelson, he didn't know of anything missing, but he said he'd do an inventory with Miss Johnson's mother. As a matter of routine we had the interior of the house photographed—and brother, let me tell you, it was a mess. I can send you the photos if you want them."

"I'd like that very much," said Punch. "Did you check on Nelson?"

"We did, and he was her stockbroker, all right."

"Give me all the information you have on him and I'll run it through R and I and see if he has a record."

After jotting down the pertinent details, Punch sat thinking, occasionally looking at the note pad on the desk in front of him. Intruding into his thoughts was the Chief's threat. Like an ocean buoy, it kept bobbing up and down on the surface, demanding his attention. He had been threatened more than once in his career, most often by hoodlums. Years ago, Mickey Levy had promised to dance on his grave.

Suddenly Punch sat up straight and wrote, APB on

Levy, on a clean page of his scratch pad. Officer Diller's report on the dead homosexual's involvement with Eva in a film and his reference to Ginger, now took on meaning. Was it a coincidence that Eva's house had apparently been ransacked by professionals? Levy and his men were, if nothing else, professional.

Punch continued to study his notes. All at once he was aware that Bonny was standing in front of his desk.

"Detective Cutler reporting for duty with Homicide." She gave him a mock military salute.

"You're kidding," said Punch.

"I'm not kidding. I was transferred from Vice to Homicide this morning. They said you were short on personnel."

Punch looked at Bonny for a moment, trying to collect his thoughts. If the Chief suspected he and Bonny were lovers, it was possible they were being set up.

"You don't seem pleased to have me in your department," Bonny said.

"I am, and I need you." He lowered his voice. "How did the transfer come about?"

"I'd finished my tour on Vice and was going to be assigned to Missing Persons when word came down from the Old Man that Homicide was short. Since I was due for reassignment anyway, they put me on temporary duty with Homicide."

"I'm delighted to have you aboard, Detective Cutler." Punch's voice was gruff, but his eyes were smiling.

"Apparently you were right about your hunch that the Johnson girl's death would become your problem."

"Yeah, but I wish I'd been wrong. There's already heat coming down from upstairs."

"There's something you should know," Bonny said. "Last night Louise busted a screenwriter named Gruzinsky for soliciting. He told her Eva Johnson stole his screenplay for *The Reckoning*, and he hated her with a passion. When I heard this morning that the Johnson girl was a homicide, I knew this might be important."

Punch arched his eyebrows with interest. "Do me a favor. Write a report with all the details about this fellow Gruzinsky. But before you do that, I want you to check out this lady." He wrote down the name, Athena Bigson, and her telephone numbers and handed them to Bonny. "She says she was Eva's maid and claims she knows who murdered her employer. Interview her. Take my car, the seat's softer." He handed her the keys.

Bonny pursed her lips and blew him a soft kiss. "I'm on my way, boss."

It was a day of travel poster sunshine. Although it had been smoggy enough downtown to make her throat sore, the air seemed to clear and cool once Bonny entered Beverly Hills. Money even buys good weather, she thought. She turned left off Hillcrest and drove up a long driveway lined with royal palms. At the end of it was a mock French Provincial villa, brick front and red-tile roof, set in a perimeter of flowering tropical shrubs.

A slim, dignified black woman wearing a uniform with a white apron opened the front door.

Bonny undid the clasp of her leather shoulder bag and lifted up the flap which held her badge, showing it to the woman. "Are you Athena Bigson?"

"Oh," said Athena. "I expected a detective."

"There are women detectives, too. Don't you watch television?" Bonny said lightly.

"I'm sorry, miss. Please come in. The people who live here are away and I'm looking after things while they're gone. I thought this would be a quiet place to talk."

Inside it was cool, everything in green and white with a vast marble foyer leading into a living room furnished with sofas the size of ocean liners. The fabric on the furniture matched draperies drawn over the huge picture windows.

"Sit down, please, miss. Can I get you a cold drink?"

"No, thank you. I'm fine," Bonny said as she lowered

herself carefully onto the couch. "Now, you said something to the officer downtown about knowing who murdered Eva Johnson. What makes you think she was murdered?"

"I read it in the papers."

"What you read was that the police are *investigating* Miss Johnson's death. Since we don't know the actual cause of death, we're looking into all possibilities."

Athena looked crestfallen. "Oh, I misunderstood."

"But let's just suppose for the moment that she *was* murdered," Bonny continued gently. "Who do you suppose would have a motive?"

Athena said nothing and smoothed her apron. Bonny registered it as nerves. She was used to honest citizens being frightened in the presence of the police. The Los Angeles black community especially had little reason to love white authority. To get Athena to talk, Bonny would first have to get her to relax.

"Perhaps you can tell me something about Eva Johnson," Bonny suggested. "What kind of person was she?"

"A good woman," said Athena.

"In what ways?"

"She always left fresh coffee for me and something in the icebox for my lunch. And even if she wasn't going to be there when I finished, she'd give me a check before she left. Sometimes when she was tired of a dress or something else, she'd give it to me. Straight from the cleaners in a plastic bag. And at Christmas she never forgot my children. She always had presents for them, and a check for me."

"What did you do for her?"

"Same as I do for all my people. Dust. Clean. Do whatever dishes are around, make the bed, water the plants. I did whatever was needed to make her house pretty and clean three times a week. And sometimes when little Vicki was there, I'd keep an eye on her, too."

"Who's Vicki?"

"Miss Eva's daughter."

"How long did you work for her?"

"Three years. I started while she was still married to Mr. Nicholas. Then when they got divorced I stayed on with her. At first I worked two days a week in the Beverly Hills house and one day at the beach, but then her mother came to stay with the child in Beverly Hills, so I worked twice a week at the beach. I guess she had her mother do the cleaning and she didn't need me there anymore."

"Did Eva have a lot of friends?"

"*She* did. Mr. Nicholas didn't."

There was a world of meaning in the answer, but Bonny decided not to follow it up at that moment. She continued asking questions in a quiet tone.

"These must seem very unrelated questions, Mrs. Bigson, but I appreciate the way you're helping out. You know, I've never met Miss Johnson's ex-husband, Nicholas. Is there anything you can tell me about him?"

Athena's hands slid down her apron again, and Bonny noticed her jaw muscles tense, closing her face like a fist. "I didn't like him."

"He must have had some qualities that attracted a beautiful woman like Eva."

"None that I can tell," Athena said coldly.

There was fear behind the black woman's eyes. She rubbed her hands on the apron again and shifted her body uncomfortably. Bonny had obviously touched a nerve. She knew she was going to have to take a chance now.

"Did Nicholas have a motive for wanting Eva dead?"

Athena's eyes brimmed with tears. "I don't know anything about any motive, but the last time I saw them together was at the beach house, and I heard him say to Miss Eva, 'I'll kill you before I let you take Vicki away from me!' "

Bonny reached over and patted Athena's hand. "How long ago was that?" she asked.

"Just two weeks ago. He'd just dropped little Vicki and her grandmother off in town and he'd come to see Miss Eva about something. I was leaving for the day—it was Wednesday—and when I walked by the bedroom, I heard them yelling. And I heard him say those words real clear."

Punch was on his way to the men's room Friday noon when he met Detective Waite carrying a large package of photos under his arm.

"The pictures from Eva Johnson's funeral this morning were just printed," Waite said. "It was a big turnout. Lucky there were two photographers with us on the job."

Punch walked back to his office with Waite.

"Any faces jump out at you?" Punch asked.

"No one with a record."

Waite set the stack of photos on the desk. The A.I.D. men had photographed every person who showed up at the chapel where services for Eva were held. Punch quickly sorted through the stack. He recognized a few celebrities, but no known criminals.

Waite laid another small stack of photos on the desk. "A.I.D. also photoed the pages with the names of the mourners who signed the guest book," he said. "Must be a couple hundred names here."

A sharp pain in the stomach almost caused Punch to double up. He gasped for breath and inadvertently put his hand on his stomach.

"Anything the matter?" Waite asked.

"Something I ate must have disagreed with me."

"I keep telling you, stay away from junk foods."

Waite was a health food fanatic, always preaching to anyone who would listen, "You are what you eat." At that moment Punch hated Waite and his goddamn health diet.

"I'll be just fine," Punch said. "On your way out, have Bonny take this list of names to R and I. Have her run them through the computer. Maybe they'll turn up something more interesting than outstanding traffic warrants."

CHAPTER *6*

R AND I WAS AT THE END OF A long, brightly lit and silent hallway in the basement of Parker Center. "Records and Identification" was lettered on one of the solid double doors. The other door, which warned "Authorized Personnel Only," opened into a small reception room where a short, chunky policewoman with gentian-blue eyes and rust-colored hair cut to regulation length was sitting at a small desk.

"May I help you?" she asked Bonny.

"I'm Detective Cutler from Homicide. I had a message Officer Soong had something for us."

The receptionist's bright blue eyes twinkled as she came around the desk with her hand extended. "Glad to see we've made it into Homicide," she said.

Bonny returned the acknowledgment. "Just a matter of time before women are in every division," she said.

The receptionist led Bonny into a room the size of a tennis court. It was all white paint and white enamel and bright overhead light. Everything seemed antiseptically clean. Banks of computers lined the walls, tended by uniformed police personnel, mostly women, who programmed

and questioned the machines in the language of compu-
terese. The room was quiet except for electronic humming
from the machines.

The receptionist stopped in front of one of the computers and introduced Bonny to a tall, slim Oriental officer
with pretty features. Officer Soong offered her hand. "We
scored a hit with one of the names you sent us," she said,
speaking with the hushed voice of a librarian. "I called
rather than send it up because I was told this was a priority
search."

She sorted through a metal basket bulging with stacks
of rip-sheets, finally locating one which she handed to
Bonny.

Bonny studied the few lines full of abbreviations, numbers and names, then handed it back to the officer. "Can you
translate this into English for me?"

"Here goes," she said. "You'd better write this down.
One of the names on the list Homicide sent down is Matt
Shaw. The numbers after his name are his New York
driver's license and Social Security numbers. He is a male
Caucasian, age twenty-eight, height six-foot-four, occupation, accountant, although at the time of his arrest he said
he was a transient staying at the Tropicana Motel, Hollywood. He was booked by BHPD on April 11, 1980, for purse
snatching. The victim was Eva Johnson, who agreed to
press charges. Bail was put up the following morning by a
lawyer named Mike Luftman. The charges were dropped.
Luftman's name was also on your list. He's clean, but
among his clients is Eva Johnson."

"Is that all there is?" Bonny asked, rapidly noting the
information.

"One more thing," said Officer Soong, reaching into the
basket for another rip-sheet. "This one says that Bud Millett, who was also on the list, was busted twice, in '78 and
again in '80, for possession of an illegal substance. I've got
his vital statistics and record here, along with the fact that

he gave his employment as 'film studio technician.' "

Officer Soong gave the computer a tender pat on its aluminum flank. "And that's all she wrote."

Punch listened and nodded occasionally as Bonny read her notes to him.

"I dunno what it all means," he said thoughtfully when she finished. He stuck an unlit cigarette between his lips. He had given up smoking when he first discovered he had an ulcer, but old habits die hard. "Just for the hell of it, check Social Security and see where Shaw was last employed and whether he's working now. Also run him through the National Crime Center in Washington."

"Yes sir," Bonny said, and left his office.

Punch's phone rang. It was one of his contacts on the Hollywood pawnshop detail.

"Just learned at this morning's lineup that you wanted any info that came in on Eva Johnson," the officer said.

"You hear anything?" Punch asked.

"A Hollywood Boulevard pawnshop owner, who also sells stones and jewelry on consignment for the hard-pressed rich, told me that last week an elderly woman brought in some items worth around a hundred thou. She said they belonged to her daughter, who needed cash in a hurry, so she was selling the stuff for her. She said her daughter was a producer at World Studios. The guy didn't have that kind of cash on hand, so he told the old lady to come back the next day. She never showed. Three days later he read about Eva Johnson in the papers and called to tip me. You want me to follow up?"

"Stay on it," said Punch, "and thanks."

Punch left his desk and beckoned Detective Bernheim to come into his office. "Have R and I check Eva Johnson's tax returns and get a TRW report on her credit," Punch said. "Also, find out where she banks and get a rundown on all the checks she's written in the last three months."

Bernheim nodded and was on the way back to his desk when Bonny rushed in excitedly.

"Got anything?" Punch asked her, rocking back in his chair.

"Guess who Matt Shaw was working for as of last week?"

"Eva Johnson's production company?"

"Evan Sadler, Incorporated."

"So?"

"Whaddya mean, 'so'? "

"What's an Evan Sadler, Incorporated?"

"It's a company that does accounting," Bonny said with a smug smile.

"Great, let me get to work."

"And among their clients are the Film Academy, and among the things they do is counting votes, and among the votes they counted are the ones that gave the Best Picture Award to Eva Johnson's movie."

"We're investigating a murder, not an accounting firm."

"Eva Johnson bails Shaw out of jail and he ends up working for the accounting firm that tabulates the Awards votes," Bonny said patiently. "Next, she gets an Award no one thinks she deserved.

"You know something, Sprout," Punch said. "You're more than just another pretty face. I think I'll go see this Sadler, Incorporated myself."

Punch let the legs of his chair touch the floor. "And before your head swells any bigger, go through the pictures from the funeral. Pull out any male Caucasians who look to be around twenty-eight years old. Damned if I know what we've got here, but it feels interesting."

For the first time that day Punch's ulcer stopped nagging him. He walked over to a pile of phone books on top of a file cabinet and thumbed through the Yellow Pages under "Accountants" until he found Evan Sadler's number. Punch intended to see Sadler, but there was one visit he needed to make first.

Punch had driven by the Motion Picture Country Home and Hospital daily for years. It was clearly visible from the Ventura Freeway, and only a few miles from his home. This time he drove through the grounds, studded with attractive bungalows set on acres of beautifully manicured, rolling lawns. People were walking or sitting on benches, some in wheelchairs with attendants.

He parked and made his way into the lobby of the main building, all stucco, stone and wood. After identifying himself, he asked the receptionist for Sally Shaffer's room.

"Room A-fourteen, the pavilion, sir, just down the hall and to your right. And would you mind signing the guest register?"

Sally, wearing a pink housecoat, was sitting beside her bed in a wheelchair when Punch walked in. Behind her was a magnificent view of the gardens through a full-length glass door. Her hair was nicely dressed, but her face showed the lines of pain and age.

"It's been a long time, Captain." Sally extended her hand and her mouth twisted to one side in a smile. "How nice of you to come visit me here."

"It's good to see you looking so well, Sally," Punch said.

"Come on, now, Captain, you should know better than to shit an old turd."

Punch laughed. "I haven't heard that expression since I was a boy."

"How are things going downtown?" Sally asked.

"I thought maybe you could help me out again, Sally."

Although she was ill and old, Sally had guessed there was a purpose to his visit. "Anything you want except the bod, Captain. That's already spoken for. But before you go on, there's a favor you could do me."

"Name it," said Punch.

"It's a beautiful day. Take me for a ride outside in my wheelchair."

"You've got it. Just tell me where you want to go."

Sally pushed a button on a console by the bed. A moment later a nurse appeared at the door. "You rang, Mrs. Shaffer?"

"Could you bring me some paper cups," Sally asked.

The nurse smiled brightly and left.

Sally turned to Punch. "Do you like sherry?"

"If you do."

"Open that closet door behind you. My knitting bag is on the top shelf and there's a bottle of sherry in it. My son smuggled it in. My doctor allows me only one glass a day, but when a handsome man comes to call, it's a special occasion. Anyway, what does the doctor know?"

Punch handed Sally the bottle, which she secreted under the folds of her housecoat.

The nurse returned with the cups and helped Sally dress warmly for an excursion into the afternoon air.

Punch took the opportunity to look around. Although the room was bright, its only furniture was an armchair and a hospital bed facing a television set suspended on brackets from the wall. Framed and autographed pictures of Sally with film greats of the past covered all the other available wall space.

When Punch first met Sally she was one of the big three Hollywood gossip columnists, along with Louella Parsons and Hedda Hopper. Punch was a rookie cop driving a radio car on downtown traffic detail when one night he pulled over a motorist driving erratically. The man, a doctor, was Sally's husband. Punch had the doctor park his car and then he drove him home.

The next day Punch received a phone call from Sally. "I want to thank you for going out of your way to be kind to my husband," she said. "Perhaps one day you'll allow me to return the favor."

Over the intervening years, Punch called Sally occasionally for inside information on certain Hollywood folk. When her husband died, Punch sent her a letter of condolence and they became friends, meeting occasionally for a quiet drink at her home after he finished work. She had retired and entered the nursing home some years ago, but Punch was sure if there was any gossip about Eva Johnson, she was the one who would know it.

When Sally was wrapped in sweaters and scarves, Punch opened the glass door and pushed the wheelchair out on the grass and toward a rose garden in full bloom.

"Now, what was it you wanted to ask me about?" Sally asked over her shoulder.

"What do you know about Eva Johnson?"

"So, the papers were right, she was murdered?" She shot the question at him.

"We're investigating the possibility."

"Of course, I'm not as much in touch as I used to be, but I've heard a few things." Sally interrupted herself. "You know, I could have been admitted to this place three months earlier than I was, instead of spending five thousand a month at some 'retirement hotel' in Pasadena, but some shitty studio secretary, two studio plumbers, and a transportation driver were on the list ahead of me. Can you imagine—*I* had to sit and wait for *them* to get admitted before they let me in? What the fuck is this business coming to?"

They reached a sign that read "Merle Oberon Rose Garden." Punch stopped and Sally surreptitiously poured some sherry into the paper cups she had been holding. Her thin white hands shook, sloshing the liquid in the cups. She toasted him. "I hope you never know what it's like to be old and dependent on others."

"Amen to that." Punch took a sip of the sweet drink.

"What do you want to know about Eva Johnson?" Sally asked.

"Anything you can tell me, for a start."

She smiled the painful, uneven smile again. "Eva was a

rare bird, a local girl, born in Hollywood. Her father, Jack Johanssen, was a producer of B westerns for the old Monograph Studios back in the forties and fifties. You weren't out here then, and most young people don't have a clue as to the mood of the country in those days.

"You have to remember, at that time America saw Russia and communism as the enemy. In 1950, Joe McCarthy was running for reelection in Wisconsin. He needed a hot issue, so he picked communism. When he turned his attention to Hollywood—because there were a lot of European immigrants in the film industry—McCarthy charged that the entire motion picture industry was infiltrated by Communists. You have no idea of the kind of terror that was generated here."

Punch listened with interest. Sally had always been able to tell a story.

"Eva's father had come from the old country and made no secret of having once been a Communist," Sally continued. "So, he was one of the first called up to testify before the House Un-American Activities Committee. Johanssen had only been a citizen a few years, and they challenged his patriotism, frightened the poor man into thinking he'd be jailed. The Fifth Amendment hadn't yet become a popular way to avoid answering a question about political affiliations. So he buckled under. He pointed the finger at some of his colleagues, and even his friends."

Sally poured herself another glass of sherry. "Am I boring you?" she asked Punch.

"Not at all," he said, although he was uncertain where the history was leading.

"Others were bullied into testifying, lots of them," Sally said. "Charges were made, friend turned against friend, colleague against colleague. People were judged without a fair hearing, let alone a trial. Guiltless people were destroyed by innuendo, although McCarthy never offered proof that the Communists had influenced even a line of dialogue in a film, let alone been responsible for one anti-American picture."

Sally crumpled her empty paper cup and dropped it on the ground. "And, God forgive me, I was one of those who went along with McCarthy without ever stopping to think that all he was really after was headlines. I know better now, but it's too late."

"What happened to Eva's father?" Punch asked.

"He was blacklisted because he'd been a Commie. And a lot of people resented the fact that he'd named names. No one wanted to know him. No one wanted to hire him. He changed his name to Johnson and worked around town as a bartender, tried to write a book, did odd jobs, that kind of thing. I think he died while Eva was only a kid."

"How do you imagine all this affected Eva?" Punch asked. He desperately hoped to find some connection between the past and the present.

Sally poured herself another cup of sherry. "Can I top yours off?"

"Thanks, no," said Punch. "I'm still on duty."

"Of course, I don't know personally what it was like growing up in Hollywood with the stigma that your father was a fink, but I'd guess it was rough. Luckily, the family had some rich relatives in the East, and Eva was sent to college there, Radcliffe, I think. When she came back, a Phi Beta Kappa, she got a job as a script reader at World Studios. From what I hear, she slept her way to the top, finally making it with David Braverman who runs the studio. That's probably how she got her first break as a producer."

Sally coughed. It was a staccato rasp, and she put a gnarled hand over her mouth. "It was my three-pack-a-day habit that got me in here," she said. "You want my advice, Punch, give up smoking before it gives you up—to the doctors."

"I'm trying," Punch said. "Tell me, what do you know about Eva's marriage to Nicholas Riddle?"

"I've heard he was a fag and it was a working partnership, which means that while they were partners it worked. Then, when she decided she could go it alone, she ended the marriage and the partnership. She got everything, including custody of their daughter. And she fired him as director of *The Reckoning*, which he'd developed. Not a nice story, but not that uncommon in Hollywood."

A withered old woman with her leg in a cast was wheeled past them by an attendant. "That's Virginia Bruce," Sally whispered. "She once had the prettiest legs in films."

"Is there anything more about Nicholas or Eva I should know?" Punch pressed her back on track.

"I heard Eva was having an interesting lesbian affair," Sally said.

"Oh, with whom?"

"Cheryl Donovan, Reese Donovan's wife. Reese had a small part in *The Reckoning*, and the affair supposedly started on location. As you probably know, Reese was arrested last Tuesday for beating Cheryl up."

Punch didn't know, but he made a mental note to check it out.

Sally continued. "Did you read today's *Daily Variety*?"

"No."

"Their reporters took a straw poll of the Film Academy members. According to them, less than ten percent voted for *The Reckoning* in Best Picture category. *Variety* wants Evan Sadler, Incorporated, who tabulates the votes, to make this year's ballots available to another accounting firm for an independent audit. Let me tell you, that's like implying the vote in the electoral college was fraudulent!"

A petite, elderly woman wearing green slacks, white canvas sneakers, and a white turtleneck sweater strolled slowly past them.

"That's Norma Shearer," Sally whispered. "She hasn't changed her hair style in fifty years. The gossip here is that Leatrice Joy has made application to come in. If she does, it'll be very interesting, because then we'll have two Mrs. John Gilberts."

"What do you think of the *Variety* story?" Punch asked.

"Personally, I doubt there was any hanky-panky because there wasn't much competition for Best Picture this year. But *The Reckoning*—" her answer was interrupted by the sharp cough—"was far and away the weakest nominee, in my opinion. The studio did spend a fortune on publicity and advertising, making a lot of the fact that the film was made by a major studio while the others were independents. That can sway the voters, most of whom have loyalty to the majors."

Sally was beginning to sound tired. Punch realized how frail her health must really be. But the tough old gal had put on a good show. With her consent, he turned the wheelchair around and headed back toward her room.

"How are they treating you here?" he asked gently.

"Wonderfully. The nurses and attendants are straight out of Central Casting. There isn't a mean one in the bunch. Most everyone else stays out of my way. They're still scared shitless of me. But you don't know what it's like to be stuck on your ass all day surrounded by physical wrecks. Two doors down from me is a miserable old fucker who refused to be interviewed on my show. I fixed him for that years ago. Before he got in here, he hadn't been able to afford a steak for years. Now he sits at the table without teeth, complaining the steaks are too tough."

"Sally, you're just as feisty as ever," Punch said as they reached her room and he wheeled her inside.

"Before you go, look into that closet where you got the sherry," Sally said. "There's some scrapbooks in there with my old columns. Take the one marked 1950-51 with you. Those are the years McCarthy was active with Hollywood. You might find something on Jack Johanssen. And one more thing. There's a dozen bottles of pills in my bathroom. Take a pill out of the bottle with a red cap and give it to me, please, with a glass of water. The glass is on the sink."

Punch brought Sally the pill and water and watched as she gulped it down. Then he pulled the huge scrapbook out of the closet.

Sally sat in her chair, eyes closed. Punch bent to kiss her cheek and she opened her eyes. "I hope it was worth the trip out here to see me."

"It was priceless," Punch said.

Successful CPA's offices the world over must look identical, Punch thought. Oak-paneled walls decorated with prints of English racehorses, large comfortable leather armchairs, pewter ashtrays. Everything contributed to the image of conservatism and substance. A matronly but beautifully groomed secretary showed him in.

Evan Sadler sat behind an oversized double partner's desk and stared at Punch's badge. Punch noticed the accountant's flushed face, his fingers drumming on the desk. Punch was silent, quite content to let Sadler speak first.

"Your office said it was urgent," Sadler said finally.

"I am investigating the murder of Eva Johnson," Punch said. He watched the color drain from the man's face; the drumming fingers now closed tightly.

"I heard she died of a heart attack," Sadler's voice was hoarse.

"The coroner's office thinks otherwise." Punch opened a manila envelope and pulled out a sheaf of photos. He placed them on the desk in front of Sadler. "Can you identify any of these men?"

Sadler flipped through the pile, putting one aside. "I know this man, but I don't recall his name."

"What can you tell me about him?" Punch asked.

"He worked here until recently."

"How recently?"

"As far as I know, he left our employ last Tuesday."

"Did he quit or was he fired?"

"He just didn't show up for work," Sadler said.

"This was right after the Awards?"

"Yes."

"And just where did he work?"

"In the mailroom."

Punch leaned forward in his chair, his big hands grasping the corner of the desk by the walnut "OUT" basket. "How long did he work for you?"

"I'd have to check the records. As I recall, he was hired temporarily about six or eight weeks ago."

"You seem to know a lot about a man who worked in the mailroom."

"I interview everyone who is hired here for any job, even janitorial."

"Since you know so much about your employees, perhaps you can also tell me, what was his relationship with Eva Johnson?"

The question and answer session, which had been progressing like a tennis match with the ball crossing and recrossing the net, suddenly came to a halt.

"As far as I know, he had no relationship with her," Sadler said carefully.

Punch noticed the thin beads of perspiration on the small man's bald head. "Do you mind asking someone in your personnel department to send up his records?"

"Why?" asked Sadler.

"Because I want to see his employment history for myself." Punch's voice was flat and hard.

Sadler looked at Punch warily, then tapped a button on an intercom cleverly hidden in an antique cigar box next to the telephone.

"Yes, sir," said a female voice.

"Dorothy, can you come in, please."

The same woman Punch had seen earlier entered the office, note pad in hand. Sadler showed her the photograph. "Do you know this man?"

She examined the photo a moment, then said, "I think he was a temp hired to fill in during the Awards period."

"Do you recall his name?" Sadler asked.

"Matt something."

"Take the picture down to personnel. Have them identify him and bring back his file."

"And anything else you have on him," Punch added.

She looked to her boss, a bit resentful at being given instructions by stranger.

"And anything else you have," Sadler repeated.

Punch took a cigarette from his pocket and put it to his mouth. Sadler pushed an ornate lighter in the form of a mallard duck toward him.

"Thank you, but I don't light them," Punch said.

The two men looked at each other in silence until there was a knock at the door. The secretary reappeared with a thin folder which she handed to Sadler, who gave it to Punch without glancing at the contents.

Punch opened the file and studied the records. The man's name was Matt Shaw. His age was given as twenty-eight. He had been hired temporarily on April 3, 1981 to work in the mailroom for four dollars an hour. He also listed his address. Another piece of the puzzle fell into place.

Punch closed the folder, handed it back to Sadler, and stood up to go. "Thank you. I'll be in touch."

As he walked out of the building, Punch had a nice, warm feeling in his belly. Shaw had given his residence as 7998 Old Malibu Road, Eva Johnson's address.

CHAPTER 7

IT WAS AN AIRLESS SATURDAY morning, already hot and humid, and bound to get worse. It had been a stifling night, and Punch had spent most of it tossing and turning, trying to assess the significance of the fact that Eva's live-in boyfriend worked at the accounting firm that declared her picture the Award winner, after which he had quit and she was killed. And the film community suspected fraud.

When he got to his office there was a teletype message from the National Crime Information Center in Washington waiting for him.

CA0194200
NO NCIC WANT DOB 070968 NAM/SHAW, MATT SEX/M
RAC/WCAUC
CA0194200
NO IDENTIFIABLE NCIC CRIMINAL RECORD SHAW, MATT

Punch removed Matt's picture from the Eva Johnson homicide case folder and studied the boyish face. Matt was just old enough to have served in Viet Nam at the tail end of the war.

He made a note to have one of his detectives check with the Department of Defense and find out if Matt had a service record.

By midday Punch's office was beastly. According to federal regulations, the air conditioner was not to be set below seventy-eight degrees, and it was already a good ten degrees higher. Punch had hung his jacket over the back of his chair and was working in his shirtsleeves, but he was perspiring heavily. His stomach hurt. Bonny had given him a plastic container of yogurt to eat, and he was ruefully considering the ingredients on the label when the telephone rang.

"I've got Levy in a holding cell downstairs," said Detective Andy Westhem. "He wants to call his lawyer."

"Let him make the call," Punch said, "then take him into an interrogation room and call me back."

Punch finished the last of the yogurt, found a donut left over by the morning shift and swallowed it as he scribbled a few notes to guide him in his interrogation of Levy.

1. What did he have to do with the homosexual beaten to death on Selma?

2. What was his daughter Ginger's relationship with Eva?

3. Where was he on the night Eva's house was burglarized?

4. Where was he during the Awards?

The telephone rang again. "We're waiting for you in two-B," said Westhem.

"Be right there," said Punch.

He took the elevator to the ground floor and walked briskly down the hall. He entered without knocking. It was a small interrogation room, just large enough to hold a battered metal desk with a green plastic top and two battered wooden chairs. Gray paint flaked off the walls. The concrete floor was chipped. The ceiling was covered with sagging, yellowed soundproof tiles. It was not an atmosphere conducive to friendly chitchat, but Levy was making the best of it. Tilted back in his chair in front of the desk, fingers laced in his vest pockets, he had a smile on his face. He's too casual, Punch thought, and determined to set him straight.

"You don't have to answer my questions, punk, but there's nothing that says you don't have to listen while I talk. And if I were you, I'd listen carefully."

Punch turned to Westhem, who was standing by the door. "Has he been given his rights?"

"He has, and asked to have his lawyer here. We're waiting for him right now."

"Why don't you leave us alone for a few minutes, Andy?" Punch said.

Levy sat up with surprise. There was a sharp clank as the legs of his chair hit the floor. "I know my rights, Captain," he said. "Without my lawyer I don't answer any questions."

After Andy closed the door behind him, Punch drew up a chair next to Levy's. He could smell the little gangster's expensive aftershave lotion.

Levy stared at him silently. After a moment he tilted his chair back again slowly. His white, hairless scalp glared like scar tissue. His teeth flashed in a smile.

Punch smiled back. "Item one," he said. "A hustler was stomped to death on Selma last week. Before he died he said he'd acted in a flick. He also mentioned your daughter's name. Item two: the movie was produced by Eva Johnson, who was murdered at the Awards last Monday night. Item three: Eva Johnson's house was burglarized the night of the Awards. The only thing missing was some rolls of film."

Punch saw fear in Levy's eyes. He had taken a long shot—that the empty film can, which he had learned of in the burglary report, had some tie-in with Levy. It looked as though the gamble was paying off. But he had very little time before Levy's lawyer would arrive. He would have to play all of his trumps at once.

"The way I see it, I can book you on suspicion of murder and probably make it stick. You had motive and opportunity, and I don't need much else. Unless . . ."

"Unless what?" Levy asked.

"Unless you level with me, and fast."

Levy sat straight up in his chair. "What do you want to know?"

"Everything there is to know about you and Eva Johnson."

"Let's talk a deal first."

"No way. You tell me a convincing story and then we'll talk. That's the only deal I'll make."

"You promise to leave my daughter out of this."

"If I can, I will," said Punch.

Levy searched Punch's eyes, trying to calculate whether he could trust him. Then he started to talk. "You remember that private club out on Topanga called Woodfield?"

Punch nodded. The club was in county jurisdiction, but he knew it well. It was the forerunner of Sandstone, a private club couples joined for a small fee and where they went, on weekends, to exchange sexual partners. Woodfield had been closed down because of a murder; a jealous husband had shot his wife and the two men she was screwing at the same time.

Levy continued. "There were cameras hidden at various places on the grounds, and some movies made. Nothing professional. Just for the enjoyment of whoever shot the film. Some of it was sent to my lab for processing. I happened to see one of the films about five years ago, and recognized Eva Johnson. She'd been on a talk show a few nights earlier. And now, there she was on film, making it with two women. Her husband, a director named Riddle, was in the background watching. I had a copy made of the negative just for future reference and put it away for safe keeping."

Suddenly the door to the interrogation room opened and a man carrying a briefcase burst in.

"Nothing my client has said until now can be used against him, and I'm going to bring charges against you for holding him against his will and forcefully interrogating him without due process!" he said.

"Out!" Levy said to his lawyer. "I'm not being held here against my will, and I'm saying nothing that can be used against me. I'm having a personal conversation with an old friend."

"You're a fool," the lawyer shouted. "You know better than to trust a cop. Keep your mouth shut and I'll have you out of here in five minutes."

"I don't want out, not just yet," Levy said firmly. "But I want *you* out."

"You heard your client," Punch said. "He came in willingly to help us in an investigation, and he'll be leaving on his own as soon as we're finished talking."

The lawyer glared at Levy. "Why the hell did you call me?"

"I call, you come. I say go, you go."

The lawyer left, slamming the door behind him.

"Go on," said Punch. "You saved the film for blackmail later."

Levy ignored the remark. "I kept an eye on Eva and her husband, and one day I read that they had separated and she had signed a multiple picture contract with a studio and was looking for new talent. I arranged a meeting with her and mentioned the film I still had. I thought she might like to have it."

"In exchange for what?"

"All I wanted was for her to give my daughter, Ginger, a part, a small part, in some movie."

"And what did she say to that?"

"She said it was a deal, but before she could give an unknown a chance in a movie, there had to be a screen test."

Levy shook his head sadly. "My daughter is a very naïve girl. No better, no worse than any other sixteen-year-old kid today. She trusted me because I set up the test. And she trusted Eva, who told her everyone does sex scenes today."

"When did you find out about the test?"

"Three weeks ago."

"Tell me about it."

"I can trust you?" Levy asked.

"You don't have any choice," Punch said.

Mickey Levy was not accustomed to being kept waiting. He sat stiffly in Eva Johnson's outer office at World Studios, light tan fedora hat resting on the seat next to him. From time to time he adjusted the crease in his trousers to avoid wrinkles. He had arrived at Eva's office promptly at 11:30 for an appointment. Now, fifteen minutes later, he glanced with increasing impatience at his watch.

"I'm certain it won't be long now, Mr. Levy," said Eva's secretary, an angular, horse-faced woman in her late forties wearing a dowdy dress and reading glasses. She had been fidgeting nervously with papers and glancing at him stealthily ever since he arrived. As Hollywood's most notorious gangster-in-residence, Mickey knew she would probably have stories to tell her friends and family for weeks to come.

"Your screen test must have come out good, sweetheart," he told Ginger over breakfast. "The producer called and asked me to come to her office."

His daughter was surprisingly unenthusiastic. "I'm not so sure I want to be an actress anymore, Daddy," she said. "Why don't you just forget about it?"

"No way you're going to change your mind now," he snapped. "Not after all the trouble I've gone through to get you that screen test." His voice softened and he smiled at his only child. "Anyway, you're a lot more beautiful than most of the stars in movies today. Ever since I saw you on stage in your class play, I knew you had what it takes to be in films, baby."

"Ohhh, Daddy," she cried, and ran from the table.

The receptionist startled Levy. "You can go in now, sir."

Mickey grunted, stood up and adjusted the Windsor knot in his tie. Carrying his hat delicately by the brim, he entered Eva's office. The office was furnished all in white, with Eames chairs and Kandinsky and Miro prints on soft white walls. Eva was smiling, but ignored his extended hand. Mickey forced himself to control his anger at the snub.

Eva went directly behind her desk, picked up a large manila envelope and extended it to him.

"The screen test came out good?" Mickey asked as he took the envelope from her.

"See for yourself. These are some prints taken from the actual film."

Mickey opened the envelope eagerly and glanced at the top glossy on the stack. What he saw stunned him into momentary paralysis. His hands trembling, he slowly turned to the second photo, then shoved the remainder of the pictures, unseen, back in the envelope. He struggled to regain his composure before he spoke.

"I could kill you for this, cunt."

"These prints are blowups of random frames. The negative is in my possession. But if anything happens to me, you can imagine what will happen to it."

Mickey shook his head sadly. "All I wanted was a break for my kid. You didn't have to do this to me. You could have said no."

"I said no."

"No, you didn't. I tried to see you through mutual friends. You were too busy. Five phone calls I made. You were too busy to return one of them. I had to get your attention somehow."

"You got it. You tried to blackmail me and now I'm returning the favor. It's a happy, balanced situation. You give me the negatives you have of me, and I'll give you the negatives of these, with my word that only one print will remain—as life insurance."

"I won't forget you for this."

"No, I'm sure you won't. Now, do we have a deal or not?"

"We have a deal, but if I were you, I wouldn't step on any cracks in the sidewalk."

Punch didn't let his sympathy stop him from pushing Levy. "So you found out who the stud in the film was and had him killed."

"I might have expressed such a wish in front of an associate or two," said Levy. "But I never ordered it."

"And you guessed that the remaining negative would be in Eva Johnson's house. So on Awards night, when she was sure not to be home, your men broke in."

"I never said that."

"You didn't have to. Nor did you have to murder Eva Johnson yourself. All you had to do was suggest it."

Levy jumped up from his chair, eyes blazing. "Do you take me for a fool, Roberts?"

"*Captain* Roberts," Punch said coldly.

"Captain Roberts," Levy snarled. "If I had murdered that bitch, do you think I would sit here and level with you? Don't you think I know there's a microphone in the wall picking up every word I say? Do you think I'd have sent my lawyer out if I was guilty of murder? You know better than that. You know you can't use what I've said in court. And there's no one to bring any charges against me. I've been nice enough to help you out. I've told you the truth, and now you can do what you want with it."

Levy subsided and sank back onto his chair.

"One last question, punk. Where were you last Monday

night between six and ten, the night that Eva Johnson was murdered?"

Levy looked directly into Punch's eyes. "As a matter of fact, I was in the audience at the Academy Awards with my daughter, Ginger. My friends told me the camera picked us up real clear."

Eva's ex-husband, Nicholas, agreed to meet Bonny at the Sports Connection in Santa Monica where he would be playing racquetball that afternoon. The smog had lifted since morning, and everything sparkled in the heat. Bonny took Olympic Boulevard out from Parker Center, thinking she could make better time on local streets than on the freeway, which began to pile up after 3 P.M., but she was wrong. Traffic was miserable. The lights were timed for a steady flow, and she missed each one. The heat and the traffic set her teeth on edge.

She was in a foul mood when she reached the huge gray structure off Bundy Avenue. Inside the building it was cooler. A pretty blond girl at the front desk greeted her cheerily and pointed out one of several racquet ball courts enclosed by thick glass walls when Bonny asked for Mr. Riddle.

There were two men on the wooden court, both wearing gym shorts and tee shirts. One of them was about forty, built like a prize fighter, and perspiring profusely. The other looked a few years younger, reminding her of a slim but effeminate Marlon Brando. He was obviously the more expert player, anticipating his opponent's shots and hitting the ball back effortlessly. After a heated rally, Bonny caught his attention. He said something to his opponent and came over to Bonny with a towel draped across his shoulder.

"You're not what I expected," Nicholas said pleasantly. "Can I buy you a fruit juice?"

Bonny nodded. He led her to a juice bar, ordered a

papaya-protein shake for himself and orange juice for her.

"Now, what can I do for you?" he asked when they were settled at a small table.

"I'd like to ask you a few questions about your ex-wife."

"She's dead. Why are the police interested in her?"

"It's policy to conduct an investigation into every suspicious death in the county."

Nicholas frowned. "What was suspicious about it?"

"We don't have the coroner's full report yet, but as a matter of routine, we've started an investigation."

Nicholas stared into Bonny's eyes. "And what does your investigation have to do with me?"

Bonny opened her purse and took out a pack of cigarettes. She put one in her mouth. He leaned forward, took the lighter from her hand and lit it for her. The gesture seemed to ease the tension between them, and gave Bonny a moment to think.

"You were overheard threatening to kill your wife," she said evenly.

"Athena." The maid's name shot out of Nicholas's mouth. "She must have listened in on hundreds of fights between us over the years. In an argument between husband and wife, lots of things are said that are foolish and lots of threats are made. But I didn't kill her. I wouldn't kill anybody."

His eyes glistened. "Look, Eva could be impossible, and there were times I would cheerfully have strangled her. But I never laid a hand on her, and I certainly didn't kill her!"

He pointed to the pack of cigarettes. Bonny offered him one. As he lit it, Bonny noticed his hands were shaking. He inhaled deeply and coughed silently.

"Does the fact that you're here to see me mean I'm under suspicion of murdering my ex-wife?"

"No, Mr. Riddle. As I told you, we're merely interviewing people who might have had cause for wanting her dead."

"You'll be a long time with your investigation then. Half of Hollywood wanted her dead, and most of them had a motive."

"Well, let's start with you, shall we?" said Bonny. "Why don't you tell me how you met, and something about your marriage."

Nicholas traced the rim of his glass with one finger, and told Bonny the story.

It had been a cold day in Manhattan and the thundershowers began without warning a few minutes before 5 P.M. Nicholas had telephoned the hotel doorman half an hour earlier to order a taxi. When he arrived at the Fifth Avenue exit, he expected to find one waiting for him. But there was a throng huddled under the awning waiting for cabs.

"I've got to check in at the terminal for the Los Angeles flight by six-thirty," Nicholas insisted.

"I'm sorry, sir," said the doorman firmly. "You'll have to wait your turn."

A husky, well-modulated voice behind Nicholas said, "If you don't mind sharing the cost of a limo, I've got one coming in just a few minutes."

Nicholas wheeled around. The voice belonged to the most beautiful blonde he had ever seen. Almost his height, she had a slim, boyish figure and was elegantly dressed. "Share!" he said. "I'll be glad to pay the whole fare myself. I've got to be on the West Coast tonight."

"Then it's a deal," said the woman, who was standing on tiptoe looking anxiously over the crowd at the street.

A black limousine pulled up in front of the hotel. "Jump in," she said.

The driver opened the car door. "Nice to see you again, Miss Johnson," he said, holding an umbrella over them both.

"I've seen you before," Nicholas said, struggling out of his raincoat.

"Yes, you have."

"Where? Studio Fifty-Four? Maxwell's Plum?"

"You're not even warm."

They rode in silence listening to the slurp of the tires on the rain-slick streets.

"I give up," Nicholas said finally. "Where have we met?"

"Later," she said. "You flying United?"

"Yes."

"Me, too."

She settled comfortably on the seat, a smile on her lips, and she was soon asleep, awakening only when the limo stopped at the airline terminal.

"We can put this on your expense account, and I'll give you half of it in cash, or we can put it on my account, and you give me cash," she said.

Nicholas was astonished. "You work at the studio, too?"

"I do. My name is Eva Johnson and I'm in project development. I know who you are. You're a contract director brought out from New York, where you directed soap operas. You've got an office on the lot, but no picture assigned yet. We were introduced once last year at the commissary."

Suddenly Nicholas remembered. They had been introduced by a mutual friend, but he had dismissed her as just another highbrow English Lit major from an Eastern college hired for the summer. More significant was the fact that she was on one of the lowest rungs on the studio totem pole and, he assessed, could not be useful to him in any capacity.

They sat next to each other on the plane. Nicholas confirmed his first impression in part. She was indeed a recent Radcliffe graduate, and she had just come to New York to attend her ex-roommate's wedding. But she was not a snobbish highbrow. She considered film a business and was using her job at the studio as a stepping stone to becoming a producer. Recently she had come across a script by a new writer about a young couple spending their honeymoon in a haunted house. She had excitedly presented it to the studio executives, who had rejected it on grounds that it was too similar to *The Omen.*

The knowledgeable way she talked about the script, however, impressed Nicholas. The story had important differences, she said; it could be made on a low budget, and it had strong box-office potential. When they parted at LAX, he promised to read the script.

The story, entitled "Haunted," turned out to be every bit as exciting as Eva had promised. Nicholas tried to interest the top brass in it. Instead, he was given a low-budget potboiler to direct. But he stayed in touch with Eva, and had dinner with her once or twice during the production of his film. The project turned out to be a disaster, and his contract was soon dropped.

He saw Eva again soon after that, and told her he planned to return to New York to pick up his career in TV.

"You want to gamble another two weeks out here?" Eva asked him.

"Doing what?"

"I've taken an option with my own money on *Haunted,* and I've gotten a rewrite. I think I can get a deal if I have a director. There won't be a lot of money in it for you, but at least it's a feature—for both of us."

"But you've never produced anything. What makes you think you can handle it?"

"You've never directed a hit, but I have confidence in you. And I have confidence in myself. I think I know where to go and how to lay it off. Are you interested or not?"

Something about Eva's certainty that she could get the film financed convinced Nicholas to team up with her. He agreed to remain in Hollywood another two weeks. Before the end of the first week, they had a deal with David Braverman at World Studios, and Eva quit her job to devote herself full time to producing the picture. *Haunted* was a

box-office success, and they were on their way as a pro-
ducer-director team.

"You haven't told me what she was like," Bonny said.

Nicholas ground out his third cigarette and considered
the ashes before he answered.

"She was beautiful and smart, a rare combination in
Hollywood."

"Is that why you asked her to marry you?"

Nicholas picked up his drink and put it down again.
Something was troubling him, and Bonny was sure she
knew what it was. Nicholas looked at his watch and then
said carefully, "I loved her."

Bonny reached into her purse and took out a printed
reply to a question she had telexed to the New York Police
Department that morning.

"In 1966," she said, "you were arrested on a morals
charge involving a male minor, and given two years probation. Before the probation period ended, you were arrested
for soliciting in Times Square. You served seven months in
jail, after which, apparently, you moved to Los Angeles.
Now this is a very important question, Mr. Riddle. Judging
by your record, I assume you were a confirmed homosexual.
How much of your past did you tell your wife?"

Nicholas held his head in his hands. "She knew everything," he said.

"She must have been a very understanding woman."

"She was more than that." Nicholas spaced the words
out slowly. "My past gave her a hold on me. That argument
Athena overheard. What she didn't hear was Eva threatening to make my past public so she could take my child away
from me."

"She must have loved Vicki very much."

"No, she resented Vicki, but she knew I loved her
deeply. Unless I agreed to her terms, she was going to take
her away."

"So you went along with Eva and hated her for forcing you to give up Vicki."

"Eva destroyed my career and ruined my life. Do you blame me for hating her?"

Bonny ignored the question. "Was there another man in Eva's life?"

"Not that I know of, and there was no other man in my life, either." His voice was tinged with sarcasm. "I know you're going to find this hard to believe, Officer Cutler, but I've changed. I haven't been interested in a man since Vicki was born. And I'm a good father—whenever they let me see my daughter. You can check my record in Los Angeles. You won't find so much as a traffic ticket."

Nicholas pushed his chair away from the table and stood. "You came here to find out if I had a motive for killing my wife. I had one, but I didn't kill her. You want proof? Get the videotape of the Awards ceremony. I was in the audience and I never left my seat."

CHAPTER 8

T HE EX-HUSBAND'S ALIBI IS airtight," Bonny said. "I checked, and the television director remembers picking him up on camera when Eva was announced as winner. Gruzinsky was also there."

"And so was Levy," Punch said morosely, helping himself to a piece of Peking duck. They were having lunch in Chinatown at General Lee's, one of their favorite restaurants. Bonny had spent the previous night at her own apartment, despite Punch's protests, because she insisted her nightmares were keeping him awake. Her wound was healing nicely, but she seemed to have suffered a psychological scar from the shooting. Punch had been busy all morning with paperwork, and lunch was their first chance to talk since yesterday.

"Three of the suspects have airtight alibis," said Punch. "I've got a hunch Evan Sadler knows more than he's told me and I want to get my hands on this kid, Shaw."

Bonny used her chopsticks deftly to pick up the last piece of duck. "Considering this is a major investigation, the Chief isn't helping you out much with manpower, is he?"

"Every division is overloaded. He just can't pull men off cases. An investigation takes time."

"Are you pleased with what I've done so far?" Bonny asked casually.

"Very," Punch said, sensing what Bonny was leading up to.

"There are a lot of *women* officers in the department who are as qualified as your men, but they're doing desk jobs."

Punch's chopsticks clattered to his plate. "Come on, Bonny, let's not start that ERA crap again. You're good and you're smart, but you're also an exception."

"I'm not starting anything, dear," Bonny said sweetly. "There're at least half a dozen qualified female officers on the street in Vice, and as many more in other divisions pushing paperwork. You say I'm doing fine, but I'm only the second woman ever assigned to Homicide."

"I've told you a dozen times, I don't think Homicide is the place for women." Punch began to feel overheated.

"The only reason you've ever given is that you don't think women have the stomach for it, that we'll puke at the sight of a bullet-riddled corpse, or we'll fold in a gun fight. Well, I didn't, and neither will the others. We're holding our own on the street, and we can hold our own in any other police assignment we're given."

"What the hell do you women want?" Punch demanded. "We've already got three times as many women on the force as we did five years ago. Why the hell do you have to push so hard? Lay back, it'll happen in time."

"No, it won't, not until we at least get a chance to fail. You know as well as I do that women establish as good or better rapport on interviews with suspects than men do. We don't come on so strong, and we're sneakier."

"Sneakier is right," said Punch. "Here we are, having a nice lunch in a nice place and you use it as an excuse for trying to proselytize."

"I'm not trying to brainwash you, Punch," Bonny said. "I just think that if your division is short, you could request a couple of female detectives."

"I didn't request *you*," snapped Punch. "You were assigned. I take whoever the Chief sends down. He's the one you should be talking to, not me."

"Maybe if you told him you were agreeable."

"Well, I'm not. So far you've done only two interviews, which may qualify you for a job on a newspaper, but not for permanent assignment to my division. I'll withhold judgment for awhile, if you don't mind."

Bonny slipped her hand into Punch's. "I don't mind, but you can't blame me for trying."

After a moment, Punch gently closed his fingers over hers. "All right, baby," he said. "You tried. Now, do you want to see me tonight?"

"Very much," said Bonny. "I'll fix dinner at my place, and you can stay with me."

"Great," said Punch. "I'm going to pay Cheryl Donovan a surprise visit this afternoon. She lives out by the Palisades. I ought to make dinner by seven."

It was late afternoon when Punch arrived at Rivas Canyon where the Donovans lived. He turned right off Sunset Boulevard, onto a tree-shaded road lined with potholes. Punch thought he knew Los Angeles well, but this winding canyon was new to him. He took in the big homes set far back from the street, the corrals, stables and riding rings. The area reminded him of the suburbs of Chicago where he grew up.

He turned into a driveway and drove past several broodmares at a trough. He parked directly in front of the Spanish-style white stucco villa with a red tile roof, and walked to the massive scarred oak front door. A TV camera mounted over the door was an obvious warning to strangers. For someone who hadn't starred in a major film in years, Punch thought, the actor seemed to live in style.

He pushed the doorbell. A female voice came from a grille by the side of the door. "Can I help you?"

"My name is Phillip Roberts and I'm with the Los Angeles Police Department. I'd like to talk with Mrs. Donovan, please."

"Can you please hold your badge in front of the TV camera?"

Punch looked up at the camera and held the badge out. As he waited for the door to be opened he studied the mares with envy. He had one old quarter horse on his acre in Chatsworth. But these were clearly thoroughbreds.

A red-headed woman about thirty, wearing a white terry cloth bathrobe that did little to obscure her lush figure, opened the door. But her face had been badly beaten. Her eyes were sunk in blue circles, her jaw was swollen, and there were contusions around the cheekbones.

"I'm Cheryl Donovan," she said, stepping aside to let him enter. "I assume you're here to talk about what my husband did to me. Not a very pretty sight, is it?"

The heavy door opened onto a cool green courtyard, off one side of which was a huge living room with rough, exposed beams on the ceiling, Spanish-style furniture, and Mexican paintings on the walls. Cheryl gestured Punch toward a leather chair and she sat down on a couch. "Now, what do you want to know?"

"Actually, I'm here to talk abut Eva Johnson."

Cheryl's face hardened. "I thought you wanted to talk about my husband. He beat me to within an inch of my life and some asshole judge lets him out on bail. What kind of justice do you call that?"

"Domestic disturbances are handled by your local police department," said Punch evenly. "I'm with Homicide downtown, and I'm investigating Miss Johnson's murder."

Cheryl's eyes widened. "Murder! Who said she was murdered?"

"The coroner," said Punch.

"And how can we help you?" a male voice asked.

Punch turned and recognized the face as Reese Donovan came into the room. Handsome, with gray hair, brown eyes, a well-preserved body in expensive casual clothes, a young man's stride. The actor extended his hand. He had a firm grip, and gave Punch a publicity photo smile showing a mouthful of perfectly capped teeth.

"This officer says Eva was murdered." Cheryl's voice had an edge of hysteria.

"I heard him, my dear," said Donovan, moving closer to his wife, who quickly edged away from him. The animosity between them was palpable.

"Eva Johnson was a friend of yours—of both of you," Punch continued.

"She was no friend of mine." The actor turned toward his wife. "She was Cheryl's *good* friend." There was a cutting edge of sarcasm in his voice.

"You bastard," said Cheryl.

"I can think of a word that might more aptly describe the two of you than 'friends,'" said Donovan. "Shall I use it?"

Cheryl stood up, tears flowing down her cheeks. She pulled the robe more closely around her. "Why don't you hear what my husband has to say first, officer," she said. "If you want to talk to me later, I'll be in my room."

Punch stood as she left the room. Donovan remained expressionless.

"Now, what would you like to know about that whore?" he asked.

"You were arrested for malicious assault early last Tuesday morning," Punch said. "Did that incident have anything to do with Eva Johnson?"

"Everything." Reese stood up and pushed his fists into his trouser pockets, pacing the room as he told Punch the story.

They were getting dressed to go to the Awards ceremony Monday night. Nominees were permitted to bring one guest, and Cheryl would be sitting with Eva in the roped-off forward section. Reese would be seated elsewhere, with friends.

Cheryl was applying the last touches of makeup at her dressing table. "You know what Eva's going to do after she gets the Award tonight?" she asked Reese.

"*If* she gets the Award," corrected Reese.

"Win or lose," said Cheryl firmly. "She's going to Barbados for a two-week rest. And you know what?"

"No, what?"

"I'm going with her."

Reese, who had been sitting on the bed pulling on his black silk stockings, stopped in mid-action. "You're what?"

"I'm going with her," said Cheryl, tossing her hair and glancing at his reflection in the mirror.

Reese stood up and walked behind Cheryl, their eyes meeting in the mirror. "You're not going anyplace without me for two weeks."

"Oh, I'm going," said Cheryl.

"Like hell you are."

"Like hell I'm not. I'm my own person, and I'll damn well live my own life. I don't need your permission one way or the other."

Rage surged through Reese's body. "As long as you're my wife you'll do what I say."

"I wouldn't put it that way if I were you, dear," said Cheryl.

"Just what do you mean by that?"

"I may be your wife—now—but that's not a permanent state of bondage."

Reese turned away and walked back to the bed, sitting down heavily, not wanting Cheryl to see that he was shaking.

"You're not going," he said finally.

"I am, and you'd better make up your mind to it."

Cheryl got up from the makeup bench and approached him. Although small and completely naked, she seemed to dominate him. "I've had it with you, your friends, and this house," she said. "I want to live, and I intend to do it before I turn into a sexless prune like the wives of your old friends. I love you, Reese, I really do, but you're out of it. Time has passed you by, and you'd better accept reality. If I divorce you, you'll never get another young thing again. So be grateful for what you have, and if you have to share me with another person, at least you've got *something*."

Reese's stomach muscles contracted as his lungs began to fight for air. "You'd better explain what you mean by *share*," he said carefully.

"You know what I mean. Eva and I are lovers."

Reese felt as though he had been hit in the stomach. "Lovers?"

"And we have been almost since that first day on location. Now, get dressed or we'll be late."

Reese stood slowly, his jaw rigid. "You bitch," he shouted. "You tell me you're a lesbian, and just like that you expect me to accept it?"

"I've taken nothing away from you, my husband. No other man's cock has entered my cunt. It's still the same as it always was, still there for you when you want it. Now be a big man and admit it could be worse, a lot worse. I could be leaving you for good, or for another man, and not just for two weeks."

Reese sagged back on the bed again. "Thank God we never had those babies."

"Don't thank God," said Cheryl coolly. "Thank me."

"The babies," said Reese, his voice hollow. "You mean you lost them deliberately?"

"That's exactly what I mean," said Cheryl.

"Cunt. Bitch. Whore. Dyke." The vitriol flowed out of Reese's contorted mouth, each word expressing the whiplash of his emotions. Then suddenly he lost control, struck Cheryl across the face, then in quick succession hit her twice more.

Emptied finally of expletives and strength, he collapsed, sobbing, on the bed, aware only of the damage he had done to the face of the woman he had, until only minutes earlier, loved with the intensity that only an older man can feel for a young wife.

Punch felt momentary compassion for the actor standing now in front of him, his expression testifying to the emotion of that night. It was difficult for any man to handle the news that his wife was leaving him for another man, but to be cuckolded by a woman must be an even more terrible blow to the ego, Punch thought.

"And what did you do then?" Punch asked softly.

"I ran out of the house and got into my car. I wanted to drive around to get some fresh air, to clear my head. My life had just come apart at the seams and I needed to be alone."

"Did you stop anyplace or meet anyone you knew?" Punch asked.

"No," Donovan said, then seemed to understand what the question implied. "Don't tell me you consider me a suspect in Eva's death?"

"You did have a motive," Punch suggested.

"I did have a motive, but I didn't kill her," said Donovan. "And I know my rights. I don't have to listen to your insulting insinuations, and I won't. You came here uninvited, and I'm asking you to leave—now."

Donovan balled his fists and glared at Punch.

"I wouldn't," Punch warned. He walked to the door and turned around. "The next time I come to see you, I'll make sure it's an official visit."

The pigeon-colored sky was turning dark gray when Bonny pulled into the driveway of her home in Laurel Canyon. She parked in the garage and stepped out of the car. Suddenly she heard a gunshot echo through the hills. A bullet thudded into the garage door beside her head.

She froze with fear for a moment, then ran to the back door of the house, flattening herself against it as she grabbed her .38 and her keys from her purse.

A second shot slammed into the eaves over her head.

Bonny struggled with the lock, tore the door open and flung herself onto the kitchen floor. She grabbed the telephone cord, jerking the instrument off the breakfast table, and frantically dialed a direct line into Parker Communications Center.

"This is Detective Bonny Cutler," she said, giving the operator her badge number and address, her breath coming in short gasps. "Someone is shooting at me!"

A "code two" was immediately broadcast. Police came from all directions painting the streets with rubber: radio cars, motorcycles, and plain-clothes units, all responding to the announcement that an officer was "down" as though their own lives depended on it. Three separate "hotshot" calls went out, as neighbors also reported a man with a gun and shots being fired.

Punch had been driving to Bonny's house from the Donovans' when he heard the code two and Bonny's address on his radio. He jammed down the accelerator. Siren blaring, he sped through the traffic.

The entire area around Bonny's house was bathed in intense light from department helicopters hovering overhead, their spotlights illuminating the hillside area from which neighbors had reported the shots. Punch skidded to a stop and dashed out of his car. He pushed his way through the group of policemen questioning Bonny. When she saw him she restrained her impulse to rush into his arms, painfully aware that they were surrounded by spectators and police.

"What happened?" Punch asked her.

Bonny repeated the story for him.

"I think you need a drink."

"Captain Roberts is right," said the lieutenant who was doing most of the questioning. "We can handle it from here on, and you'll be around if we have any further questions."

Once inside the house, Punch embraced Bonny. "There, there," he said. "Nothing happened."

Bonny pulled away from him. "What do you mean, 'nothing hapened'? Someone took three shots at me!"

"But he missed and you're all right. That's all that matters." Punch leaned over and kissed her lightly. Bonny closed her eyes. When she opened them again she saw Punch's eyes were wet. She fingered a tear on his cheek.

"I love you," he said hoarsely.

She squeezed his hand. "I love you, too."

Punch poured her a scotch and waited until she had taken a gulp. "Do you think you were followed home from downtown?" he asked.

Bonny shook her head.

"That means someone knows where you live and was waiting for you. The question is, who?"

"I haven't a clue."

"Have you busted anyone on Vice recently who might have it in for you?"

Bonny thought a long moment. "I can't think of anyone. Louise said that screenwriter—Gruzinsky—was pretty nasty when she flashed her badge, but I've never had much trouble."

"Well, we'll get whoever it was," Punch said. "But that reminds me I want to check Gruzinsky out."

CHAPTER *9*

G̲RUZINSKY LIVED NEAR THE top of Mulholland Drive on the edge of Beverly Hills. Punch was driving on Beverly Glen Boulevard toward Mulholland when he heard fire engine sirens coming up behind him. He pulled over to the side of the road and stopped. A red and white ambulance, followed by a fire truck, raced past him. The driver of a car several lengths ahead of him had ignored the sirens. Dumb sonofabitch, Punch thought. If the medics were responding to an emergency call from a heart attack or accident victim, seconds could be the difference between life and death. Punch passed the car and glared at the elderly man behind the wheel.

Gruzinsky's address was in an elegant new housing development overlooking the San Fernando Valley. It was a dazzling day, the view from the top of the mountain clear for miles. However, a thick trail of black smoke creeping down into the basin threatened the perfection of the scene.

Punch turned into one street and realized that the fire was at Gruzinsky's address. Skidding to a stop in front of a yellow-slickered fireman holding back the gathering onlookers, he flashed his badge and was waved on through. Firemen in front of Gruzinsky's handsome townhouse were pouring water into the charred garage, which was still giving off acrid white and yellow smoke. Medics wheeled a gurney holding a body covered with a tan blanket toward the ambulance.

"What the hell happened here?" Punch asked the fire captain, a tall, slim man with an Irish face and a salt-and-pepper military mustache.

"Best I can figure out before the arson boys arrive is that the guy who lived here was making some free-base in his garage and apparently blew himself up. But it'll take days to sift through the rubble and find out. Judging by the chemical residue in the garage, my hunch is that I'm right."

"Anyone else inside?"

"Not that I know of. Neighbors say he lived alone."

"That him on the gurney?"

"It is," the captain said.

Punch walked over to the ambulance, which was about to leave. He flashed his badge. "Mind if I have a look at the victim before you leave?" he asked the medic in charge.

"What's left of him, you mean," the medic said.

Punch stooped over and crawled into the back of the ambulance. He carefully unsnapped one of the canvas belts holding the body down. A medic lifted up the blanket. Punch almost retched. The entire upper body of the man on the stretcher was burned beyond recognition.

The interior of the garage was in ruins, but the townhouse itself was still intact. Punch made his way into the living room, a high-ceilinged space, beautifully decorated with seventeenth-century French and Spanish pieces. There, a slight film of ash and the odor of smoke were the only tangible evidence of the fire.

Punch questioned some of the neighbors. Everyone had heard or felt the shudder of the explosion a few minutes after two that afternoon. Edward M. Meyers, a retired New York advertising executive who had recently moved next door, had telephoned the fire department immediately. An installer for Theta cable who had been working inside Meyers's home had attempted to get into the garage but was driven back by smoke and flames.

As Punch walked back to his car, the fire captain was wrapping it up. "If we gave this investigation priority, how soon do you think we could find out what really caused the explosion?" Punch asked.

The fire captain fingered his mustache. "I'll try to get back to you sometime tomorrow."

Back at his office, Punch found a telephone message: "Call Coroner Dahlstrom." As he dialed the number, Punch looked out the window at the New Otani Hotel. The red wind sock was limp.

"What's up, partner?" Punch asked Dahlstrom.

"S.I.D. ran some tests and found some minute fragments of plastic and powder embedded in the Johnson girl's vital tissues. They're going to run some soft tissue X rays later today, but—get this—they theorize she was killed by an internal explosion."

"A what?"

"You heard me, an internal explosion."

Punch whistled softly into the phone. "How would that be possible?"

"Undoubtedly she ingested something which somehow exploded and blew out the aorta. That's all I know for now."

The deputy coroner sounded pleased with himself.

Punch took out the Johnson file and studied it. He thought for a moment. Then he closed the file decisively. Tomorrow he would pay Evan Sadler another visit.

When Punch entered Sadler's office unannounced, the middle-aged secretary looked him over coldly.

"Do you have an appointment with Mr. Sadler?" her voice was hostile.

"Just tell him Captain Roberts is here on an urgent matter."

"He's in conference," the secretary said.

"Either he cancels the conference or I do."

The secretary thought a moment, then pushed a button on the telephone. "Captain Roberts insists on seeing you, Mr. Sadler. He says it's urgent." Then, "Mr. Sadler will be right with you," she said, not looking at Punch.

The office door opened, and three men carrying attaché cases filed out. Punch entered the office before the last man out could close the door.

Sadler was behind his desk. "What can I do for you this time, Captain?" he asked.

"I hope you can answer a few more questions," Punch said.

"If I can." Sadler sounded weary.

"One: this boy Shaw was arrested several months ago for stealing Eva Johnson's purse. Two: his bail was paid by her attorney," Punch said, ticking the points off on his fingers as he spoke. "Three: he then goes to work for you in your firm's mailroom. Four: the address he gave on his employment record was hers. Five: she wins an Award no one expects her to get. Six: she is murdered. Seven: he quits his job and disappears from sight." Punch stared intently at Sadler. "Now, one could say this is all coincidence, but you're an accountant. What do you suppose it all adds up to?"

Before Sadler could gather his thoughts, Punch slammed his hands on the desk, making the accountant jump. "Now, why don't we stop playing games, Mr. Sadler, and you tell me what his job entailed."

"Just what are you investigating, Captain?" Sadler asked.

"Murder, Mr. Sadler. I don't give a rat's ass about any hanky-panky relating to your accounting procedures—unless they have some bearing on my homicide investigation. Which they may."

"Do I have your assurance that what I tell you will be held by you in the strictest confidence?"

"I can't make any such deal and you know that," snapped Punch. "But I will tell you this. If this man Shaw's involvement with your firm has nothing to do with the murder I'm investigating, whatever else you may tell me will remain confidential."

Sadler inhaled deeply a few times before deciding to tell Punch the story.

Three days before the Awards were announced, Will Thomas, Sadler's chief accountant, came to him around midday to tell him about a discrepancy he had discovered: two of the envelopes that contained ballots had identical numbers, which was unlikely since the numbering was done by a sophisticated computer.

"There's nothing to do but check the Academy and find out the names of the voters who received these two ballots," Sadler said. He studied the two envelopes on the table, his nose quivering slightly as though they gave off a bad odor. "We'll need to find out how both voted, so their choices can be tabulated correctly."

"I've already found one was sent to an actor, now retired," said Thomas.

"Good work. And have you contacted him?"

"No, sir. Not without your permission."

"Then do so at once. I'll listen in on the extension."

Sadler sat, small fingers laced under a fleshy but pink and well-shaven chin, while Thomas dialed the number. Sadler had been one of the first certified public accountants in Los Angeles. He had founded the firm which bore his name and now had three hundred employees; its reputation rested on one word: integrity. Never in the history of the firm had there been a breath of wrongdoing associated with him or any one of his six partners.

It was a source of annoyance to him that each year, in the month of April, his firm received prominent mention in the press as official custodians and tabulators of the ballots mailed directly to his offices by the 3,500 voting members of the Film Academy. Such publicity was not in keeping with the low profile he felt his firm should maintain.

Thomas gestured with his hand. Sadler picked up the telephone. A thin, aged voice said, "Maguire at your service."

"Mr. Maguire, this is Will Thomas from Evan Sadler, Incorporated. We tabulate the Awards ballots for the Academy."

"Yes."

"I wonder if you can help me?"

"Try me."

"I have a favor to ask of you. It's somewhat irregular, but . . ."

"Speak up. I don't hear so well anymore."

"Do you recall getting your ballot from us this year?"

"I sure do."

"Did you, by any chance, receive more than one envelope? Perhaps two envelopes, one inside the other?"

"One, just like always."

"Then I have a favor to ask of you, Mr. Maguire. As I said, it's somewhat irregular, but I can assure you it's quite legitimate."

"You want a favor, I want a favor."

"Of course."

"Send me some pills."

"What kind of pills?"

"Any kind," the old man on the phone wheezed.

"What I mean is, pills for what kind of ailment?"

"I mean, *any* kind of pills. There's nothin' that isn't wrong with me. Any pills for anything will suit me fine." The voice lowered confidentially. "Of course, pills for female ailments don't apply."

"You will have the pills, sir, you have my word on it. Now, you said you only filled out one ballot?"

"Right."

"And do you recall how you voted?"

"Hah. Of course I do! There's little enough for an old

fella like me to do night after night but to see movies. I saw
them all, took notes on 'em. Spent two hours filling out that
ballot just like always. It's the only way I have left of staying in touch with a business I worked in for fifty-odd
years."

Thomas put the double-numbered ballots on the table
in front of him and read off the list of nominees in all cate-
gories, asking Maguire how he had voted. Both ballots tallied exactly with the old man's memory—except for one
category—Best Picture. He had not voted for *The Reckoning*.

"The same thing happened when we checked out the
other ballot." Evan Sadler made a cat's cradle of his fingers
and stared at it thoughtfully.

"Quite a yarn," Punch said.

Sadler took a deep breath, reached into his desk drawer
and brought out a five-page memorandum stamped "Confidential." He handed it to Punch, explaining that the last
paragraphs on the second page were especially relevant.
The memo detailed the procedure his staff was to follow as
official tellers for the balloting of the members of the film
community. Punch studied the last paragraphs silently.

> In addition to maintaining complete secrecy until the
> Awards are presented, we must also take responsibility to
> see that only members of the Academy in good standing cast
> ballots which are included in the tabulations. Ballots are to
> be mailed in specially printed envelopes which have our
> return address on them; thus an improperly addressed
> envelope will be returned to us and not to the Academy,
> where it would escape our control.
> The address on the envelopes must be checked against an
> approved list of Academy members, which will in turn be
> verified by reference to the Academy's records of paid-up
> members. (As the regular auditors for the Academy, we will
> check the accuracy of the Academy's records each year
> during the course of our audit.)
> Along with the official ballots, the envelopes mailed to the

members should contain return envelopes addressed to us and identified through a special numbering system. That is, each return envelope must carry a number which corresponds to a number on the official list of members in good standing. In this way, we can be certain that envelopes returned to us are those which were mailed only to members in good standing. We do not accept ballots sent to us in any other manner.

"For more than twenty years, the procedure you just read has been followed to the letter," Sadler said. "It was foolproof. Or so we thought."

Punch handed the memo back to Sadler. "And what did you do when you discovered someone had found a way to beat your system?"

"We reported the discrepancy and were instructed by several network executives and representatives of the Film Academy not to make this public. Since we are governed by their contract, and not vice versa, we complied. And the Awards were presented as usual."

"Did you investigate the discrepancy any further?" Punch asked.

"Of course I did. But the woman in charge of the mail-room had been with the firm for more than twenty-five years and was above suspicion, as were most of my other employees. Then I remembered that one of the mailroom staff had been on sick leave for several weeks, and had been replaced by a new employee, Shaw, whom I had briefly interviewed myself, as I told you. When I learned that Shaw had failed to show up for work Tuesday morning, I felt certain he was the culprit."

"Fascinating. And what did you do then?"

"I hired a private detective to find him."

"And?"

"He learned that Shaw had cashed his paychecks at a grocery store in Hollywood. His last check is still uncashed. The detective has a man staked out at the store, waiting for him."

"Then what does he plan to do?"

"I want Shaw brought here to me for questioning," Sadler said.

Punch smiled. "So far so good, but *I* want Shaw for questioning in a murder investigation. Bring charges against him later, for fraud, if you wish, but only after I'm done with him."

"If you arrest him will his involvement with the Awards also become public?" Sadler asked.

"At the moment, I'm interested only in his relationship with Eva Johnson and his possible implication in her death. I don't see that your business with him is my concern."

Punch got to his feet. "Now, if you'll give me the address of the grocery store you mentioned, I'll take over from here."

"I'd be grateful if you'd keep me informed," Sadler said miserably.

"I'll do that, Mr. Sadler."

CHAPTER *10*

Punch amended his original APB on Shaw to include round-the-clock surveillance of the Hollywood grocery store where he had cashed his last two salary checks from Evan Sadler, Incorporated. Shel Diller was temporarily assigned to Robbery Homicide at Punch's request. On Wednesday morning, Shel and rookie Charles Bloch had been waiting in the tiny, cluttered manager's office for six hours when the store's cashier signaled them that Matt had come in.

The men swooped down on Matt like two hawks, one on each side, pinning him against the counter. "We're police officers," said Diller. "We'd like to talk to you."

Twenty-five minutes later, Matt was booked at Central Jail on suspicion of murder.

"I knew you'd get me a suspect," the Chief boomed out. He offered his hand to Punch, who was always surprised at the man's limp grip.

"That's all Shaw is, sir," said Punch flatly. "A suspect."

"Did he have anything to do with the sniping at Officer Cutler?"

"We're looking into that right now."

"Good." The Chief nodded approvingly. "And how is Officer Cutler doing?"

Punch shifted his weight uncomfortably and decided the best thing to do was to play it cool. "When I last saw her, she seemed fine. It frightened her, of course. But she's a pro."

The Chief nodded. "Good that she wasn't hurt. The papers blew the story all out of proportion. They said she was working on the Johnson investigation; they even gave her address. They're getting a memo about that. They should know better than to publish an officer's address."

There was silence for a moment. The Chief looked pensively at his hands. His fingers were long but fleshy, Punch noted, and freshly manicured.

"One thing puzzles me, though," the Chief said. "I've read the report on the incident. She didn't fire back."

"She had her weapon out," Punch said, "but she called for backup first, rather than attempt to find a sniper in the hills alone."

The Chief blew some air out in a long aspirant sigh. Punch knew there was more to come.

"Have you interrogated Shaw?" the Chief asked.

"I'm going to do it personally as soon as I leave here." Punch was relieved at the change of subject.

The Chief rocked back in his chair, framed as always, between the state and federal flags. He unclasped his fingers and tucked them into his vest. A smile spread over his handsome face. Punch was startled. The Chief didn't look like Walter Pidgeon anymore. The web of wrinkles around his eyes was gone. His skin was smooth. My God, he's had an eye-lift! Punch thought. He'd been told that the Chief had been out a few days with a "cold," which was why he hadn't been on his back recently.

"Something the matter, Roberts?" the Chief asked.

"No, sir, I was just thinking of how well you look."

Partial transcript of the first three-hour taped interrogation between Captain Phillip Roberts and suspect Matt

Shaw at Parker Center, Los Angeles, April 15, 1981, approximately 9 A.M. Suspect's rights were read and waived by
him.

Q. Do you know why you're here?

A. No.

Q. You've been booked because I think you had
something to do with Eva Johnson's murder.

A. Oh, shit. Murdered! Oh my God. Hey, man, I didn't
know she was murdered! I'm the last person in the
world who wanted her dead. I loved her! And I was
set for a part in her next picture!

Q. When was the last time you saw her?

A. I was out front watching the Awards on TV when I
saw her drop. I ran around to the back of the theater,
but the cops wouldn't let me near her.

Q. Why don't we start from the beginning? Tell me how
you first met Eva Johnson.

A. I was out here from the East looking for a break,
you know, looking for exposure as an actor. On
Friday night, the first week in February, I heard
there was a screening at the Director's Guild
Theater. I figured there was no better place to be
seen, so I tried to crash it, but they stopped me at the
door. Back on the street I saw this blonde park a
Ferrari. It was a knockout, and so was she. I watched
her go into the theater and figured she was an
actress. When I walked by her car, I noticed her
purse was on the seat and the door was unlocked. I
was going after her to tell her, but then I figured it
was her problem, not mine. So I kept walking. But I
kept thinking about that purse on the seat. Like I
said, I was tapped out and after a few minutes I
figured, why not? I'd never ripped anything off
before, but this looked like a cinch. I'd just opened
the car door and picked up the purse when she came
back, saw me, and started screaming. I didn't know
what to do. I was frightened. So I dropped the purse
and started running. Then two cops happened along
and busted me. Next thing I knew I was at the police
station in cuffs, booked for burglary and as a

transient. I spent the night in the tank.

Q. And then?

A. The next morning, Saturday, they told me I'd been bailed out. I couldn't figure out who'd gone bail for me, because I didn't know a soul in town. But when I walked out the door, she was there in the Ferrari waiting for me.

Q. What did she say to you?

A. That her lawyer had done some checking on me, and this was my first offense. She said she hated to see a nice young man like me go to jail.

Q. What did you think?

A. I figured I'd lucked out, that she was one of those fancy Beverly Hills rich broads you read about in novels. You know the kind. Someone interested in new action.

Q. What made you think that?

A. I noticed her eyes when they were patting me down. She looked me over pretty good, like she was measuring me for size, if you know what I mean.

Q. I know what you mean. What happened next?

A. She asked me how I'd like to drive out to the beach with her and maybe we could talk.

Q. And then what happened?

A. It's a long story.

Q. We've got plenty of time, son.

As they drove out toward the beach in silence, Matt noticed Eva glancing at him from time to time. When their eyes met, an electric charge seemed to travel between them. She stopped at her house in Malibu, showed him around, and they spent the afternoon on the beach. She wore an old UCLA sweatshirt several sizes too large, and a pair of blue jeans rolled up just below her knees. They tossed a frisbee and chased each other up and down the beach. Once he tried to kiss her and she pulled away, saying, "There'll be time for that later."

When they returned to the house a large, muscular woman wearing a white smock was in the living room, waiting by a portable massage table. Matt went upstairs to Eva's bedroom. He showered and lay down on her bed for a short nap. When he awoke, the room was half dark. Eva was standing in the doorway. He had never seen anyone more beautiful. Her blond hair hung softly around her face. Her eyes were a brilliant blue, and a sheer white diaphanous gown clung to her body.

He reached toward her. Still she stood there, eyes cast down. Then she slowly came over and perched on the edge of the bed. He could see a tiny pulse beating in her throat, and the puckering of her nipples. He felt a stirring within him, and the soft warm touch of her hand completed his erection. He reached up to turn her face toward him. She drew the gown over her head and, moving quickly, straddled him. Then, her hand guiding him, she lowered herself onto him. She was dry, and penetration was difficult. He began to kiss and caress her breasts. Finally he was inside. Almost immediately he shuddered and climaxed. "Damn!" he said, "I'm sorry. I just couldn't hold it."

Her look was contemptuous. She raised her body off his and walked toward the bath. Stopping in the doorway, she turned and studied him. "You've got the equipment all right. Now you've got to learn how to use it. Get dressed. We're going out for dinner and start on your lessons."

They drove in uncomfortable silence down the coast highway. Matt tried to make conversation, but Eva's eyes were fixed on the road and she was unresponsive. They passed through Venice. She turned toward the Pacific, parking in front of Land's End, a French bistro set incongruously on the edge of the beach. The restaurant was dimly lit, and a slim, fashionably dressed young man greeted Eva with an embrace.

"Have you got a table for two on this side, Enrique?" Eva asked.

"Anything you want, Eva," he said, guiding them to a small secluded table already laid with a white linen tablecloth, a basket of French rolls, and a ramekin of pâté.

They ordered white wine and sand dabs. Matt still tried to make conversation, but Eva was silent and only smiled occasionally. After the dishes were cleared, she moved her chair alongside his. Feeling the tips of her fingers making a circular motion over his crotch, he looked at her in amazement.

"Start talking to me," she ordered.

"Are you crazy? With you doing that?"

"You heard me. Talk."

He felt himself beginning to swell as her busy fingers increased their pressure. He gasped as she tugged his zipper down and reached inside his pants, grasping his testes.

"Start talking," she said. "If you give any clue to what I'm doing, I'll get up and leave you here."

He tried to push her hand away, but she grasped him so hard it made him wince. "Relax," she ordered, lightly running her fingernails over his tumescence.

Matt started to reach a climax. "I'm going to come," he whispered through clenched teeth, as the waiter arrived for their dessert order.

"We'll both have flan," said Eva coolly. The waiter nodded. At that moment, Matt came in spurting waves. Eva smiled at the departing waiter, covered Matt with a napkin, and told him to wipe himself dry.

"Now we'll go back to my place and try again," Eva said when they finished dessert. "And this time you'll wait for me to come, even if you have to wait all night. I'll make a lover out of you yet, big boy."

Matt had been to bed with dozens of girls, but, as Eva reminded him later that evening, he hadn't had any real women. That night was a milestone in his sexual maturity. He did as she ordered until she was finally satisfied. He fell asleep, exhausted, only to be awakened after what seemed only a few minutes.

"I've never been able to sleep all night with anyone," she said. "Why don't you go downstairs and sleep in the room off the kitchen?" Then she kissed him lightly on the mouth, the only part of his anatomy her mouth had missed during their lovemaking.

In the morning she came into the kitchen as he was fixing coffee. She was wearing a bikini. Without makeup she looked like a teenager. He went to kiss her, but she avoided him.

Q. Whose idea was it that you move in with her?
A. No one's. It just happened.
Q. If you were her boyfriend, as you say, how come you didn't take her to the Awards?
A. We were talking about it, but a few days before the Awards, she said it was over between us. She told me to move out.
Q. How did you feel about that?
A. Hey, I never expected it to last. She never promised me it would. She promised I'd be in her next picture, and while I was with her she treated me pretty well. Any way you look at it, I was ahead.
Q. I asked you how you felt about being told to get out.
A. I felt lousy, but I figured maybe she'd change her mind.
Q. You weren't angry?
A. I was hurt and a little pissed off. But those are the breaks. Like I said, we'd had a good run. I had no complaints.
Q. Just how pissed off were you?
A. I don't know what you mean.
Q. Well, I think you were pissed off enough to want to kill her.
A. You're crazy, man!
Q. Well, the way it looks to me, you had a motive for wanting to kill her. And right now you're the prime suspect. Think about that. I'll see you tomorrow.

As Punch walked back to his office, something troubled him. The kid had been a virtual volcano of voluntary information. He was too candid, too open. In Punch's experience, the only people who talked so much without prodding and prompting were usually hiding some dark area of their lives that the interviewer had missed. He intended to have another go at Matt soon.

He had been back in his office only a few minutes when a call came in from Dahlstrom.

"Those spooks in the bomb squad scored a hit," Dahlstrom said. "They put those bits and pieces I dug out of the Johnson girl through every conceivable test, and they found some fragments of what appears to be a mini-battery, along with the shards of plastic I told you about.

"Their computer has come up with a projection of the probable size and shape of what they think was a small capsule. The inside of the plastic shell had a streak of conductive ink, which probably functioned as an antenna. And they've found traces of an explosive. It was from the azide family, most likely lead azide. They theorize that she was killed by a small bomb that she ingested, probably thinking it was a pill of some kind. Whoever put it together was a fucking electronic genius."

With his free hand, Punch searched through his top drawer for a bottle of aspirin. "What's that you said about an antenna?"

"I'm no expert on this kind of business," Dahlstrom said, "but I just heard that one of the government spooks from Phoenix is here in L.A. for the day on business. The bomb squad boys say he's a top authority on clandestine devices. He tells you not to start your car, you'd better evacuate the block. I tracked him down for you and gave him all the info. He's willing to stay in town a coupla hours longer and meet with you, if you can make it tonight."

"Tell me where and when," Punch said.

The Santa Monica pier was deserted. It was too early in the season for tourists, and the curio shops, go-cart rides, and arcades that lined the boardwalk were dark. Only one restaurant, The Lobster Catch, was open. The wind was blowing a storm in from the Pacific, and the early evening air was chill and damp. Punch stood in front of the boarded-up merry-go-round, impatiently checking his watch. The bomb expert was already fifteen minutes late.

A car stopped a moment as though the driver were looking over the pier. Punch automatically noted the make, model and year. He was not surprised when, a few minutes later, he heard the sound of footsteps coming from the alley behind him.

"Evening," said a voice from the shadows. "Sorry I'm late, but the traffic was heavy."

Punch grinned. His contact had stopped his car on the street to survey the situation, then parked and come up from behind. A professional himself, he appreciated that quality in others.

Bill Rogers was about ten years older than Punch and four inches shorter, with a slight paunch that Punch guessed was mostly muscle. He had a moon-shaped face, a ruddy complexion, and was almost bald, perfect casting for a benevolent uncle or Santa Claus, except for his eyes. Behind his steel-rimmed glasses they were riveting—gray, unblinking, and expressionless. This is a very tough man, Punch thought, as they walked side by side across the boardwalk to the restaurant, the tapping of their shoes and the shrieking of gulls the only other sounds in the night.

The restaurant was almost empty. Without discussion, the men chose a secluded booth overlooking the ocean. Rogers spoke first. "I was on my way to Oxnard for a convention, which is why I suggested we meet here."

"I'm grateful you could find time to fit me in," Punch said.

They made small talk about police business and friends in common until midway through dinner. Rogers, apparently satisfied with Punch's credentials, brought up the subject of the bomb.

"Why don't I recap my conversation with the coroner for you?" Rogers said. "There's no doubt that Eva Johnson was killed by a mini-bomb that she ingested in the form of a capsule. Dahlstrom's people were right. They'd already discovered that the inside of the capsule had traces of conductive ink, which was undoubtedly the antenna. They know the explosive was in the azide family, and I'm sure it will turn out to be lead azide, which is sensitive enough to be initiated by a low energy source.

"It's also a powerful explosive and one that can be easily bought. And they've found fragments of a battery. All you need add to these things is a miniature radio detector plus a remote trigger mechanism—and you have a damned efficient bomb."

"What would make it go bang?" Punch asked.

"It probably received frequencies in the microwave region, that is, several thousand megacycles per second. That permits a short antenna a few centimeters long designed to respond to a signal of a certain frequency from the transmitter."

"What about the transmitter? How would it operate?"

"Chances are, the output of the transmitter would be no more than a few milliwatts, suggesting a small device that should fit nicely in an attaché case or—think about this—it could be as small and thin as a woman's evening bag. Flick a switch or push a button and—superburp!"

Punch's next question was one which had bothered him since the first indication that a bomb had killed Eva Johnson. "Why wasn't there any noise?"

"There undoubtedly was, but it was probably muffled by the body. And since it was only a minute amount of explosive, the sound was probably no louder than a cough."

"Have you ever come across such a device?"

Rogers peered over his glasses at Punch. "No. But I've already spoken with the experts who make these special little toys for the government, and they say it's feasible."

"I'd say it's a lot more than feasible, it's *happened*," said Punch. "Is there anything you can tell me about the components of the bomb? Where would they come from?"

"Any competent chemist or even a smart college chemistry major could make you a small amount of lead azide from readily available materials. But most likely it was removed from a blasting cap filched from some construction operation, storage magazine, or a stump farmer's barn. As for the device itself, anyone skilled in electronics and explosives could put it together. You can buy conductive ink in most any radio shop. As for the transmitter, my eight-year-old son built an amateur radio transceiver himself last year from a kit."

Punch was deep in thought. "How far away could the transmitter be from the bomb itself and still set it off?" he asked morosely.

"Probably no more than a couple of hundred feet. My guess is that the person was in the audience or just inside the building, so he or she could turn on the transmitter to send the signal that would activate the bomb."

Punch shook his head. "What kind of person do you think we're looking for?"

There was a faint smile behind Rogers's eyes. "I'm not a detective or a psychiatrist, but whoever designed this package would need an electronics background and, well . . . let's just say I'd want him on my side."

CHAPTER *11*

P UNCH ARRIVED EARLY FOR HIS three o'clock appointment with David Braverman at the Polo Lounge of the Beverly Hills Hotel. The maître d' measured him with a glance and decided he was worthy only of a booth by the bar, rather than one in the more secluded area to the rear of the lounge.

Punch knew the Polo Lounge well. As a young detective working the organized crime detail in the fifties, he had been there often to look over the turf. Like Perino's, Chasen's and La Rue, the other "in" places for show people of the day, the Polo Lounge was just another snobbish hangout as far as Punch was concerned.

Although it had been years since he had last been there, it seemed to him that time had slipped gears in the perpetual gloom. Plastic plants and plastic people. The faces were the same, only the names had changed. He noticed a cocaine buy taking place at the bar between two rock-singer types, but ignored it. That was for the Beverly Hills PD to worry about.

"Captain Roberts?"

Punch looked up and nodded. A tall, handsome, middle-aged man offered his hand. "David Braverman," he said, sitting down stiffly opposite Punch. Bad back, Punch thought.

"What can I do for you?" Braverman asked.

Punch took out his wallet and flashed his gold badge. "I'm investigating a murder, Mr. Braverman, and I want to ask you some questions."

"Ask away," Braverman said.

The waiter set down a large bowl of guacamole dip and potato chips. "Nice to see you again, Mr. Braverman," he said. "The usual?"

"Yes, please," said Braverman. "Will you join me in a scotch on the rocks, Captain?"

"Make mine Irish on the rocks."

"Now, what would you like to know?" Braverman asked pleasantly.

"We have reason to believe, Mr. Braverman, that Eva Johnson was murdered at the Academy Awards ceremony." Punch paused and then added, "I understand you were more than just her employer."

Braverman's smile slipped sideways, and red began to show around his collar. "I don't know where you heard that, Captain."

"From a very good source," said Punch.

"Your source was mistaken."

Punch shrugged. He leaned over the table toward the producer. "We have two ways of doing this, Mr. Braverman. We can have a nice, pleasant chat here, or we can go downtown. Now, what'll it be?"

Braverman reached into the inside pocket of his jacket. Punch's hand dropped to his belt where his .38 was holstered. Braverman saw the move, paused, then slowly and deliberately withdrew a cigar. He put it in his mouth and lit it, his eyes never leaving Punch.

"And what will you charge me with, Captain?"

"As a suspect in the murder of Eva Johnson."

Braverman smiled. "You know you can't make that stick."

"Maybe not, but I'll have you in the tank overnight.

And I promise you won't see your lawyer until tomorrow morning. By then you'll also have the press on your ass."

Braverman exhaled a thin trail of smoke and sighed. "All right, Captain, have it your way."

"Why don't we start with your telling me how you first met her?"

In 1977, Bella Abzug had come to Los Angeles to gather support for the Equal Rights Amendment. David himself was neither for nor against women's rights. His view was that if women were entitled to anything, they usually got it. But Bella Abzug, with her ridiculous hats and strident speech, was bound to be fun. Besides, the gathering was being hosted by Jane Fonda, whom he was courting for a film.

The people at the party had been attractive and intelligent and he found himself signing a check for two hundred dollars as a public relations gesture.

When the political part was over, the guests retired to a patio offering a depressing view of the smogbound city. Clustered around an open bar and tables, they plied themselves with drinks and hors d'oeuvres. He was nursing a vodka on the rocks in a plastic tumbler, his eyes seeking out Ms. Fonda, when a remarkably beautiful young woman in her late twenties, tall, sensuous, with a high, youthful bosom and hair tied in a ponytail appeared at his elbow.

"Hello, David Braverman, I'm Eva Johnson," she said, offering him her hand. She had a surprisingly firm handshake, he noted, and her voice was husky and well-modulated. A would-be actress, for sure.

"We've never met," she said, "but I have a script I'd like you to read. I've called your office several times, though you've never returned the call. That's not nice, you know." Her mouth formed a cute pout and her eyes, wide and jewellike, were smiling. He recalled seeing her name on the daily list of calls his secretary kept for him.

"I'm sorry," he said, trying to sound sincere. "But I've been very busy."

She laughed. She had a deep, rumbling laugh, unexpected in a girl so slender and carefully put together.

"And you didn't know who I am," she said. "But perhaps now that we've met more or less formally, you'll accept my next call? Now, tell me what brought *you* here?" she asked, sipping her drink, her eyes mocking.

"I came for the waters," he said, in a poor imitation of Bogart in *Casablanca.*

"But there are no waters," she said, feeding him Claude Rains's line.

"I was misinformed."

They both laughed. "I must have seen that picture twenty times, and if it was on tonight, I'd be home watching it," she said.

"Quite a picture," he agreed. "And Bogie was quite a man."

She was standing close to him now, and he could smell her tartly sweet perfume. She looked at him thoughtfully over her raised glass. "You know, Mr. Braverman, even if you don't return my calls, I think I still like you."

Two days later he saw her name on a list of telephone calls. In the space marked "message" his secretary had written, "Play it again, Sam" and penciled in a large question mark.

He dialed her number. When she answered, he lisped, "Hello, sweetheart," in the Bogart style.

"You called back," she said happily.

"There's no one else I can practice my Bogie imitations on."

Her laugh was uninhibited.

"About that script you have for me," he said.

"You name the time and the place and I'll bring it to you."

"There's no point your coming in with the script," he said. "I won't have time to read it while you're here. So why don't you just send it to me at the studio, give me a couple of days with it, and then we'll talk."

"Fine," she said. He thought he detected a note of disappointment in her voice. "I'll leave it with your secretary tomorrow and call you at the end of the week."

The script arrived the next day. Expecting the worst, he gave it to his secretary to read. Her memo came in the next morning: "A well-crafted melodrama with believable and sympathetic characters who, on their honeymoon, become involved in a haunting that has all the elements of *The Omen,* and the spookiness of *The Exorcist.* My personal opinion is that this could be a low-budget sleeper and you should read it for yourself." He did.

Two days later Eva called and they arranged a meeting. Eva arrived punctually, wearing a pale blue silk shirt-dress, the color of her eyes. She gave off an aura of vitality and sex that seemed to fill the room. As he rose to greet her, he noticed she had exquisite legs.

A man followed her in. Pale and thin with a brooding face, a young Marlon Brando. Probably the writer, he thought, but when they were introduced, he recognized the name Nicholas Riddle. He had read something about him in the trade papers.

"You liked the script," Eva said at once to Braverman.

"I did. It needs some work, but it's a good story. And what role do you fancy for yourself, Miss Johnson?"

"You'd better call me Eva if we're going to work together, David."

He admired her bravado.

"I want to be associate producer so I am close to the production from its inception," she continued. "For that I want a fee, and I want Nicholas to direct."

"What kind of money are we talking about?"

"Fifty thousand dollars for me, and a hundred and fifty thousand for Nicholas."

"That's a lot of money for a woman who has never produced and a man who has never directed a feature film."

"Let's be forthright about this." She smiled significantly. Her voice grew the tiniest bit softer. "You know what I want. I know what you want. It's right here in this room, all of it. The package could be more interesting than it appears on paper."

Braverman raised his eyebrows. He looked at Nicholas for an embarrassed instant. The young director was wearing the same thin smile he had had on his face when he entered the office.

Eva rose from her chair and approached him, close enough so he could feel her body heat. Hands on hips, her back to him, she began to study one of his framed prints. The sun streaming through the window shone through the thin dress, outlining her long straight legs.

"We're talking about a total financial outlay of two hundred thousand dollars for fees, plus script," she said, turning slowly to face him.

Incredible, he thought. She thinks she can get a deal by just turning me on. "The script has been turned down all over town," Braverman said.

"Not so. It was passed on by one studio, and I liked it so much I quit my job there, took up the option personally, and borrowed the money for a rewrite. It's a good script. Otherwise we wouldn't be here right now. So let's make it easy on both of us.

"You know that ten percent of a film's budget should easily cover the cost of director, story rights and producer. This film should cost out at two million five, so I'm in the ball park with fifty thousand left over for the script and rights. Give me half for the option, the other half the day we go to photography. That way you'll be on the hook only for the option money, plus whatever you are required to pay Nicholas to start preparing the film. I'll withhold my fee until you give us a firm go-ahead. And perhaps by then we'll have reached a greater 'understanding.' "

"What do you want to start preparing?" he asked Nicholas, who looked at Eva to answer for him.

"Let's say twenty thousand dollars, which makes your initial exposure fifty thousand," she said.

The offer was fair, verging on generous.

"All right," he said, "you've got a deal."

Nicholas stood up, shook hands with Braverman, and left the office. Eva stood directly in front of Braverman. "I think we're going to have a very interesting relationship," she said, and gave him a full kiss on the mouth, leaving him with its memory.

"So you kept the deal with her?" asked Punch.

"I did more than that," said Braverman. "Although I hadn't personally produced a picture in years, I decided to make an exception on this one."

"And that's when you and Eva started your affair?"

"Do I have to tell you everything?"

"I appreciate your cooperation. I'm sorry if it's painful."

"Only painful now."

Braverman beckoned to the waiter, holding up two fingers. Within moments, two more drinks were on the table.

"You must understand something, Captain," Braverman said. "People outside the film business think most decisions are made on the casting couch level. That may be true in some cases, but not often. And it never was true with me. Not until I met Eva. I had been happily married for twenty-seven years, and I tell you this in all honesty, I never cheated on my wife, not once in all those years."

"Eva must have been something for you to break that kind of record," Punch said.

"She could have had any man she wanted, but she said she wanted me. She knew all about my wife. But she said she'd settle for me part-time. The perfect mistress. No demands, always accommodating. No jealous scenes."

Punch could see Braverman's eyes glazing a bit.

"I'd forgotten how exciting a love affair could be. Those months with Eva were the most memorable of my life." Braverman looked disconsolately down at his drink. "After all, I was old enough to be her father. But I thought she really loved me. I suppose I was really just an old fool."

"How long did the affair last?"

"Two years."

"And she never caused you any grief?"

Suddenly Braverman looked up, and fear showed in his eyes, fear and something else. Punch decided to press the issue. He sensed he was onto something.

"I'm not interested in your personal or professional life, Mr. Braverman, apart from my investigation. But it serves my purposes to find out what kind of woman she was; how she operated with people. Maybe you can shed some light on that?"

Punch noticed Braverman's brow furrow and a slight tic in his right eye. "You must have had arguments at one time or another," he continued. "What were they about?"

"Is our conversation confidential, or will it be used against me later?" Braverman asked.

"If you had nothing to do with Eva Johnson's murder, then what difference would it make? I just want to know how she handled her relationships with people close to her."

Braverman shut his eyes for a moment and leaned back in his chair. His voice was soft when he spoke, "All right Captain, I'll tell you." He took a swallow of his drink. "*Haunted*, Eva's first picture with Nicholas, was a modest success, so I signed her for *The Reckoning*, but without Nicholas. The trouble started about midway through production."

"What the hell is this Porsche doing on my budget?" Eva demanded, waving a budget sheet in front of Braverman's face. "Two days before filming and a Porsche creeps in."

He looked up, startled. This was the first time she had abused her prerogative as his mistress.

"Why shouldn't it be a Porsche?" he asked. "Would you rather it was a Honda?"

"As a matter of fact, I would. The Porsche is on the books for thirty thousand dollars. You can buy any car you want straight out and not charge it to my picture."

"What else can I charge it to? Besides, that's not any of

your business, is it? All you have to worry about is making your film."

"I've also got to worry about making a profit."

"If you don't like my getting a little token, okay. When this whole picture is over, you can have an accounting firm audit the books. Everybody does that. We expect it. Of course your accountants are going to find things we have done that they don't consider appropriate. And we'll make a settlement. *We* know that. *You* know that. *They* know that. So why are you getting excited about it? That's the way it's done. Money gets money. So be grateful I'm only taking a finder's fee—instead of a percentage."

"Are you saying that you got a kickback on every picture you were involved with?" Punch asked.

Braverman shook his head vigorously. "Not a kickback, a perk. A little something extra, when it can be squeezed out of the budget. It's common practice."

"If it's such common practice, then why are you making such a point of it?" Punch asked.

The lurking fear was back behind the eyes. Braverman picked up his drink and put it down again. He looked at his watch.

"You're trying to tell me something, Mr. Braverman," Punch said. "What is it?"

"You wanted to know how Eva operated. Well, I can tell you she was not above blackmail."

Three days before the Awards, Eva's agent had telephoned Braverman to ask if he had okayed her deal for a third picture. David had replied flatly, "No way."

Just before lunch that same day, his secretary announced over the intercom that Eva was there. "Tell her I'm out!" he said, just as the office door burst open and Eva came in.

Braverman, who had once thought Eva the most beautiful and exciting woman he had ever known, now viewed her with the eyes of a man confronting an ex-wife demanding a raise in alimony. He felt only despair that he had given her the right to claim anything from him.

"Hello, David," she said. Her voice was cool and flat. He noticed that she toyed with a long gold necklace that hung down to her waist, and thought with satisfaction that she too was tense.

"Have you had a chance to look over the contract?" she asked.

"I have."

"And have you signed it?"

"No."

She arched her eyebrows and sat down in the leather chair in front of his desk, crossing her legs to reveal an ample amount of bare brown thigh.

"Why not?"

"I told you weeks ago that there is no way I can justify giving a relatively inexperienced producer autonomy on a film with a ten million dollar budget."

"But my last two pictures have made money. And one of them is now up for an Award."

"The aggregate budget of your last two pictures was under ten million. And you know as well as I do, the fact that *The Reckoning* was nominated is a credit to your publicity campaign, not the picture."

"It may win an Award."

"It may, but I strongly doubt it. And whether it does or not is a moot point. The fact is, I can't okay the deal you want."

"You *can't* okay it, or you *won't*?"

"Won't."

"I see. You know, you don't leave me many options."

"You can always go to another studio with your picture," he said, a tinge of irony in his voice. He knew through the grapevine that she had already submitted the package to other studios and been turned down.

She was momentarily silent. Then she said, "I really

wanted to make it here." She paused. "In fact, I intend to make it here."

"Not while I'm studio head." Braverman couldn't control the vehemence in his retort.

"Perhaps you won't be studio head much longer."

"You know something I don't?"

"No, but I know something the trade papers, the stockholders, and the IRS might like to know."

"Oh?" He felt blood rushing to his head. "And what's that?"

"I know how you get kickbacks on every film produced on the lot. I know all about double-entry bookkeeping, and how the studio accountants skim from profits money that is supposed to go to the producers."

"Blackmail?"

"You can call it what you will."

Her tone reminded him of the night they broke off their relationship, and she called him an old man trying to find his youth with a young woman.

"You know what happened to Cliff Robertson after he blew the whistle on David Begelman. Begelman went on to bigger and better things, and Robertson had trouble getting jobs. You forget one thing about this industry. It may be venal and cutthroat, but we protect our own."

"That's a chance I'm willing to take, David. The question is, are you willing to take it? All I've ever wanted was a chance to produce a big-budget picture, and to get a chance, you sometimes have to take one."

"And you'd destroy me to get it if you had to?"

She stood up. "You have until Monday to call my agent and okay the deal. If I don't hear from him, and I get on stage Monday night, I'll tell the world about you and your nasty little operation. And if I don't win the Award, I'll hold a press conference Tuesday morning and you'll be finished in this town. Now, think it over. Either way, I'll cut your balls off."

Eva leaned over the desk and kissed his forehead. "Think it over," she said again.

He watched her walk out. When the door closed, he picked up a ceramic ashtray and flung it across the room, watching with satisfaction as it bounced off the wall and smashed into pieces.

He knew Eva well enough to believe her threat. It reminded him of a practice once popular on an island in the South Pacific, in which a man guilty of adultery with the wife of a chief would be taken to a field where a stake, the height of his scrotum, was planted in the ground. The adulterer would stand at the stake, and a small wooden pin would be driven through his scrotum. A wood pyre was then built around him and set on fire. The woman with whom he had committed the act was permitted, at the last minute, to throw him a knife before he was incinerated.

Braverman had little choice. If he allowed her to blackmail him once, he would be in her pocket from then on.

When he left the office, he dropped by the prop department on his way to lunch. He intended to borrow a gun.

Braverman looked tired and worn. It had taken a lot of guts to tell a cop the story, and Punch appreciated that. But he was still a cop. He stood up and shook Braverman's hand.

"Thank you for leveling with me, Mr. Braverman. But do us both a favor. Don't leave town without letting me know first."

Punch leaned back in the big redwood hot tub he had built himself and closed his eyes. The heat penetrated his muscles and he relaxed. He sat up on an elbow at the tinkle of ice cubes. Bonny, wrapped in a bath towel and carrying martinis, handed him a glass as she cautiously sat on the edge of the tub opposite him, dangling her feet in the water.

"This is my idea of heaven," Punch said, looking up at

the night sky. "Funny how you never see stars downtown, but twenty-five miles out, the air is crystal clear."

Bonny smiled and tickled his toes with hers.

"How soon do you think you can get in the tub again?" Punch asked.

"This week, but it'll be another ten days before the wound heals completely." She took a sip of her martini. "Was it my bullet that killed that man?"

Punch avoided her eyes. It was a question he had been anticipating for days. That morning he had learned that ballistics had matched up the bullet in the dead robber with Bonny's gun.

"The people in ballistics think so," he said.

"If it was really my bullet that killed that man, I'm quitting the department," Bonny said.

"No, you're not," said Punch. "Don't forget, they were trying to kill us."

Bonny shuddered. Punch stood and enfolded her in his arms. "Honey, I know what you're going through. I've been through it myself. Every officer who takes a life feels guilt and remorse and invariably wants to quit. But it's part of the job. And chances are you'll never have to use your gun again. Meanwhile, I've arranged for you to see the department shrink. Talk it out with him. Then, if you still want to quit, it's your choice."

"Did that man have a family?"

"No," said Punch. "He was never out of jail long enough. He had a rap sheet as long as your arm, and spent two-thirds of his life as a guest of the county."

"Who do you think tried to kill me?"

"I don't know yet. It could have been someone you busted on Vice. Or it could have been one of the people you interviewed on the Johnson case. Or, maybe it was just some crackpot. I've got Waite and Bernheim on the investigation full time. They'll come up with something."

Bonny brushed her eyes with the back of her hand. "How did it go tonight?"

"Do you want to talk or make love?"

"Can't we do both?"

Later, while they lay in each other's arms on a redwood chaise longue on the patio, Bonny asked him how his meeting with the government agent went.

"It looks like Eva Johnson was killed by an explosive device that she somehow ingested," Punch said.

Bonny's eyes widened. "How the hell . . . ?"

"A mini-bomb the size of a pill. Getting her to swallow it is no problem. The problem is that the device could be exploded at any time by anyone anyplace within a couple of hundred yards of the Pavilion. That means most of the alibis of the people we've interviewed don't hold water.

"So far, everyone we've seen had a motive for wanting Eva dead, and most of them were in the Pavilion that night. If the government spook is right, anyone of them could have triggered the bomb from a transmitter as small as a pocketbook."

"Who are your main suspects?"

"It's a real rat's nest," said Punch. "We know that Eva Johnson's mother was trying to pawn jewelry. Maybe to get money to pay off Mickey Levy, who could have been blackmailing Eva, or maybe to cover up a bad investment. We do know that Eva tried to blackmail Levy, who was at the Awards with his daughter Ginger. I've had the telecast rerun, and Ginger was carrying a purse which could have held the transmitter to trigger the bomb. Eva was also blackmailing David Braverman, the head of the studio, who was also at the Pavilion. He admits to getting a gun and wanting to kill Eva, but we know she wasn't killed by a gun. Reese Donovan has no alibi for that night, and he certainly had a motive for wanting Eva dead. But according to his story, he didn't know his wife was having an affair with Eva until the night of the Awards.

"Matt Shaw was responsible for rigging the Awards, and Eva had booted him out of her life, so he had a motive. He claims he was in front of the Pavilion watching the show on an outside monitor. Furthermore, her ex-husband Nicholas hated her because she took their daughter from him and did him out of a film. He was in the audience. Evan Sadler seems to be clear so far, but he was backstage at the Awards with his wife. And he was carrying a briefcase."

Bonny suddenly sat up and looked down at Punch.

"What is it, honey?" he asked.

"You remember we saw *The Reckoning* together when it first came out?"

"Yeah, I do."

"It was about a boy who sees his father murdered in front of him, and grows up determined to get vengeance?"

"Yeah," said Punch, puzzled.

"Later, after we left the theater, you told me that most policemen live with the fear that out of their past, out of all the enemies they might have made, one of those people would one day demand a reckoning."

"I'm with you," said Punch.

"Well, it seems to me that your investigation so far is of all the people in Eva's *immediate* past. Maybe you haven't gone far enough back? Isn't it possible that somewhere along the way, like years ago, she did something to someone who has had it in for her for a long time? Or, maybe her father or mother did something to someone, and she paid for it." Bonnie sank back on the chaise. "It's just a thought," she said, "probably a silly one at that."

CHAPTER *12*

Punch was at Kirsten John-
son's front door a few minutes before nine on a cloudless
Good Friday morning. Kirsten had just returned to the
house after seeing her granddaughter off to visit a friend.
She was washing up the breakfast dishes when the door
chimes sounded.

Punch flashed his badge and identified himself. "I'd
like to talk with Mrs. Johnson," he said.

"I'm Mrs. Johnson," Kirsten said. "You could have
called and arranged for an interview."

"I was in the neighborhood," Punch said, noticing that
she had a touch of a European accent.

Mrs. Johnson reluctantly asked him in. He was surprised at how little resemblance there was between the lithe
elegant blonde whose murder he was investigating and this
big-boned, middle-aged woman, almost six feet tall, her
gray hair pulled back and tied severely in a bun. She led the
way into the living room.

"I was just going to make myself some coffee," she
said. "How do you take yours?"

143

"Black, please," Punch said gratefully. He had not yet had his first cup of morning coffee.

Kirsten pulled her gray woolen sweater down over her broad hips and left Punch alone.

He scanned the room professionally. It was a large room with huge dark oil paintings of pastoral scenes on the cream-colored walls. The newly covered furniture was bulky, old-fashioned, and comfortable, with fabric sleeves protecting the arms. Fresh-cut flowers in ornate crystal vases rested on lace doilies on heavy tables. Even the lamp-shades were from another period, large and bulky, some with tassels. It reminded Punch of his childhood in the Mid-west, the kind of room middle-class families of European heritage used only for important guests and state occasions: funerals, visits from the local clergyman, entertaining their child's schoolteacher.

Mrs. Johnson reappeared carrying a tray with white porcelain service. She placed a cup and napkin on the coffee table in front of Punch. Her hand shook slightly as she poured the coffee. Nerves or age? he wondered.

She sat down stiffly on the couch. "Now, what did you want to see me about?"

"Did your daughter have any enemies?" Punch asked bluntly.

"Why do you ask?"

"Because we have reason to believe she was mur-dered."

Kirsten put her hand up to her mouth to stifle a scream, then soon began to sob quietly. Her body rocked back and forth.

Punch's sympathy yielded to the pressure of the inves-tigation. "I'm sorry to tell you this way," he said finally, "but the coroner is certain of his findings."

"How?" Kirsten sobbed.

Punch decided the details would be only more upset-ting. "I'm not sure," he said, "but there's little doubt in the coroner's mind."

"Did she die in pain?"

"No," said Punch. "It was instantaneous."

"Thank God for that," said Kirsten. She made an effort to pull herself together. "Who did it?"

"We don't know, which is why I'm here. I hoped you might be able to help me. Do you know of anyone who might have wanted to kill Eva?"

Mrs. Johnson tried to blink tears away from her eyes. "None that I know of. But you must understand, I knew very little about my daughter's life. She was a very private person."

"Was she being blackmailed?"

"Not that I know of. Why do you ask?"

"Because a Hollywood Boulevard pawnshop owner remembers you bringing in some valuable jewelry to sell the week before Eva's death."

"Eva gave me some jewelry as a gift," Kirsten said. "I needed money, so I decided to sell it."

"The pawnshop owner said that you told him you were selling it for Eva."

Kirsten looked directly into Punch's eyes. "I said that because I was sure he'd wonder where I got such expensive jewelry." Her eyes never left Punch's face.

She's lying, Punch thought. But the jewelry could wait.

"What can you tell me about Eva's childhood?" Punch asked.

Mrs. Johnson relaxed a little. "She was a very beautiful little girl, more of a tomboy than most of her friends, and very good in school. She never caused her father or me any problems."

"What was he like?"

"Johann came from Sweden to Hollywood when he was a teenager, and worked in the film industry as a producer for most of his life. He died when Eva was fourteen. She was in junior high school."

Punch sipped his coffee thoughtfully. "I understand that Mr. Johnson testified before the House Un-American

Activities Committee. Did that have any effect on Eva?"

"That was a long time ago. Is it necessary to dredge up that awful history again?"

"I think it might be useful."

Mrs. Johnson sighed. "Were you in Hollywood in the fifties?"

"No," said Punch.

Kirsten patted her skirt down on her lap and sat up very erectly, reminding Punch of his grandmother who also came from Europe.

"When I was a girl living in Norway under the Nazi occupation, we were all afraid of only one thing—the knock on the door in the middle of the night when we would be taken away without explanation because somebody decided we were guilty. When it happened in our neighborhood, friends looked at each other suspiciously and stopped being friends. That is what it was like here. We were all afraid that somebody would point at us and say something that Senator McCarthy or his committee thought added up to conspiracy or treachery. We all waited for the finger of accusation, the knock on the door in the middle of the night.

"Johann had been a Communist back in the early forties, and he admitted it before the committee. He'd left the party, but they still kept after him to rejoin. Once he admitted the truth to the committee, they pressured him to name the people who tried to recruit him. He did. And then he was finished in the industry. Luckily, we had some investments and we lived on them until he died. Then Eva and I lived on his life insurance."

"Did his testifying have any effect on Eva's life? I must ask you this again."

"She was only an infant when the hearings took place."

"But she grew up his daughter in Hollywood. Surely it must have affected her childhood somehow. What about her friends, or friends' parents?"

"I don't see what all this has to do with my daughter's

death." Her face was livid with strain, but her voice was firm.

"Please understand, Mrs. Johnson," Punch said, "your daughter was murdered. You do want to help us find her murderer, don't you?"

"Of course I want to help, Captain. But I don't see how what her father did can have any bearing on his daughter's death thirty years later. What Johann did was not so unusual. Of the hundred or so witnesses who appeared before the committee, more than a third named names."

"You told me of the climate of Hollywood during the investigation," Punch said. "What was it like later? I've heard of the Hollywood Ten who went to jail for taking the Fifth Amendment, and were later cleared of the charges made against them. Surely there must have been some backlash against the people who informed?"

" 'Informing' is a bad word, Captain Roberts. Johann was a foreigner who became successful here, and adopted this country. He loved America. As one of the first called before the committee, he thought he was being patriotic by cooperating. He had no idea—none of us did then—that the committee was on a witch hunt."

"Then there was no reaction against him? You said he lost his job at the studio."

Mrs. Johnson clasped her hands in her lap and was silent a moment. "You want to know what it was like for Johann, Captain?" she said finally. "All right, I'll tell you. It was hell. Many stars and writers refused to work with him because he had testified. He felt that everyone had turned their backs on him. He became ashamed of going to public places where he might see someone he once knew and be snubbed. Mostly he stayed home trying to write a novel, though he'd never been a writer. And he began to drink more and more until he died. The doctor said it was cirrhosis of the liver, but I know he died of a broken heart."

Again a long pause before she continued. "We went

out for Eva's tenth birthday to the Brown Derby. She had never been there, and Johann was proud to show off to her the place where he'd had so many lunches with famous people whose pictures were on the wall.

"A man came in with his son, a few years younger than Eva, and sat at the next booth. The man saw Johann and said loudly enough for everyone to hear, 'Another booth, please, I don't sit next to that fink.' 'What's a fink, Daddy?' Eva asked my husband. Johann told her it was not a nice word. Eva asked what it meant, so Johann tried to tell Eva what had happened in Hollywood, and what he did for that man to call him a name. It happened that man was one Johann had named, and his career, too, was ruined. Johann understood why the man hated him, but he could not explain it to Eva."

"What was the man's name?" Punch asked.

"Does it matter now?" Mrs. Johnson asked. "He's dead. Let the past die with him.

"As for Eva . . . everyone who is successful makes enemies. Eva was strong-willed and determined. She lived for success. But since she was twenty and graduated from college, I've known little of her friends. She left me alone with my memories, and I became her housekeeper and her accountant."

Mrs. Johnson began to rock back and forth again, and there were tears in her eyes.

"I'm fishing, Mrs. Johnson," Punch admitted quietly. "I'm looking for someone out of the past who might have hated Eva enough to kill her. Perhaps someone whose career was ruined by Johann's testimony?"

"I don't think anyone really held it against Eva. Oh, in the beginning, there were some girls in Eva's class whose parents refused to accept her in their homes because she was the daughter of an ex-Communist who had also testified. But when she was at college she met a girl whose father had been named, and they became good friends. Later she met the son of Johann's lawyer, and they worked together."

"What was his name?"

"Gruzinsky," Kirsten said. "Elliott Gruzinsky."

"You know, Sprout, you may have said something last night." Punch was sitting behind the desk having a cup of coffee with Bonny. "Apparently there were some people in Hollywood who hated Eva Johnson's father for naming names before the McCarthy committee, though I doubt they'd murder his daughter for revenge. The one thing that did come out of my interview with the mother, though, was the fact that Elliott Gruzinsky's father was old man Johnson's lawyer."

Punch put an unlit cigarette in his mouth. "There may be some connection there. Let's follow up on it."

"What do you want me to do?" Bonny asked.

"Start with R and I. See what the computer has on Johnson or Johanssen. You'll probably come up dry, unless he had a criminal record. The next step is the Academy of Motion Picture Arts and Sciences library. Chances are they'll have good coverage of the McCarthy period. What you're looking for is the names of the people Johnson identified as Communists. Then we'll run a check on them."

Punch grinned at Bonny. "It's a long shot, but it was your idea. So you're elected."

Partial transcript of the second three-hour taped interrogation between Captain Phillip Roberts and Matt Shaw at Parker Center, Los Angeles, April 17, 1981, approximately 2 P.M.

Q. How're they treating you here?
A. Shit, man, I'm in jail! But I haven't been beaten or buggered. Not yet, anyway.
Q. You've been treated okay then?
A. Yes.

Q. No complaints against us? This is for the record, you know. This is all of your own volition.

A. No complaints.

Q. Fine. Now tell me, how long were you in Vietnam?

A. Almost three years.

Q. What was your rank?

A. Technical sergeant when I was discharged. But most of the time I was a corporal.

Q. What unit were you with?

A. Explosive Ordinance Division.

Q. What was your job?

A. Mostly we defused land mines, Viet Cong incendiary devices, booby traps. Sometimes I worked with the spooks who assembled the bombs. You know, helped with the wiring, that sort of thing.

Q. Did you ever make bombs?

A. No, they were mostly assembled before I ever got to them. My specialty was disassembling.

Q. Do you know how to make a bomb?

A. Sure, pipe bombs, Molotovs, simple stuff.

Q. You say you didn't have anything to do with Eva's murder, but I can build a solid case against you just on circumstantial evidence. You had the motive and access, and the necessary technical background to make the device that killed her.

A. What do you mean, technical background?

Q. She was killed by a small bomb in her stomach.

A. You gotta be kidding! That's not possible!

Q. And you know bombs.

A. The only bombs I know how to make are the ones any kid in high school can put together. But a bomb like that, I don't—

Q. I'd like to believe you're innocent, Matt. I really would, because I don't want to send an innocent man to trial, but—

A. Goddamn it, I *am* innocent! How often do I have to tell you before you believe me?

Q. Do you know Elliott Gruzinsky?

A. (long pause) I think I met him once with Eva. There was some problem between them. Something to do

with the picture she was making, but she never said
what it was.

Q. You met him only once?

A. That's right.

Q. How did you feel after Eva kicked you out?

A. I told you, I was hurt and teed off, but she never
promised me a rose garden. She lived up to her end
of the deal so I had no complaint. I guess I thought
what we had going was more than it was.

Q. Was Eva bisexual?

A. Hey, man, no way!

Q. Did she ever take any drugs?

A. Yeah, she took pills, lots of 'em every day—vitamins,
uppers sometimes, blues, and sometimes reds. But
she wasn't a pill junkie if that's what you're getting
at.

Q. Who was her supplier?

A. She got it on the set.

Q. From who?

A. Shit, I don't know. Every film set has a pusher.
That's not my scene, man, so you're asking the
wrong person. (Long pause) Oh, my God.

Q. You just thought of something. What was it?

A. Nothing. I didn't think of anything.

Q. Then what was the "Oh, my God" about?

A. Nothing.

Q. Now, you've thought of something you don't want to
talk about. That's the most interesting thing yet, in
light of all the things you're willing to talk about.
"No, I didn't do this. No, I didn't do that, I'm not
capable of murder." Suddenly one thing occurs to you
and you don't want to talk about it. I'm trying to
save your life and you're holding out on me.

A. (Inaudible. Long pause)

Q. All right, let me see if I can think of why you don't
want to talk about it. You've just come up with an
answer to one of those questions I asked you. So all I
have to do is figure out which of them might have
elicited that response from you.

A. I don't want to talk about it.

Q. Let's see. You were saying that the only bombs you knew about were simple ones, and you were talking about drugs. You said "Oh, my God," which meant you thought of something you hadn't considered before. Otherwise you sure would have brought it up earlier, because you're liable to spend the rest of your life in the slammer for a murder you say you didn't do. Do you think you're insane?

A. No!

Q. Well, you may be, because instead of helping me prove your innocence, you're doing everything to make me think you guilty. Now, if you didn't kill Eva Johnson, who do you think did?

A. (Silence)

Q. Boy, you don't understand. Your life is on the line and I'm the only person in the world who can help you save it. Now, what was the "Oh, my God"?

A. Nothing, really. I just kind of blanked out.

Q. You flashed on someone. Who was it?

A. No one.

Q. Tell me again, what was your job at Evan Sadler, Incorporated?

A. I worked in the mailroom.

Q. Whose idea was it that you rig the Award for Eva's movie?

A. (Long pause) How do you know about that?

Q. We know a lot about you. Now, tell me, whose idea was it, yours or Eva's?

A. I want to be fair.

Q. So be fair, but don't try to shit me.

A. I don't really remember whose idea it was. Soon after we met we were talking one night about the Awards—by then I knew she was a producer. She said the studio had spent a fortune on ads, and her picture had just barely gotten the nomination. But she didn't think it stood a chance in hell of winning. I asked her how the Awards were decided. She gave me a copy of a bulletin describing the tabulation process. I read it and said I thought they'd covered everything except for one item. Some clerk in the

mailroom could probably fuck up the whole
procedure.

Q. Did she suggest you might be that clerk?

A. No, not then. A few days later she told me she'd
heard Evan Sadler, the accounting firm, was hiring
temporary help. She offered me a deal. If I got the
job and could work my way into the mailroom and
was able to do anything for her with the Awards,
she'd give me a part in her next picture. Well, like I
said, I didn't have a job, and I liked her. I really liked
her. If I could do something for her, I would, and the
promise of a part in a film was a big bonus. So the
next day I went down to Evan Sadler, phonied up an
impressive background, and applied for a job. It
happened there was an opening in the mailroom, and
I pushed my way into it. From then on, one thing led
to another, and I figured out the routine.

Q. What was it?

A. It was my job to open the envelopes containing the
ballots, which were sealed in another envelope. I
noticed that the envelopes and ballots always had
identical numbers. And I figured all it would take to
win an Award in any category was about five
hundred votes. So one day I swiped about five
hundred of the blank ballots and the envelopes they
were to be sealed in. Then I had a friend who works
for a printer run off the same numbers on my
envelopes and ballots as were on about five hundred
of Sadler's.

Every lunch hour I was left alone in the mailroom.
When I opened ballots that came in, every time I saw
one that had the same number as one of mine, I
copied down all the same votes on one of my ballots,
except that I always put an X next to *The Reckoning*
as Best Picture. Then I would bring my ballots up to
Accounting to be tallied.

Q. What did you do with the original ballots?

A. I took them home with me and burned them. Hey,
how did you get onto me in the first place?

Q. You slipped and sent Accounting two identically

numbered ballots. That started them checking.

A.   I guess I goofed. That must have been the day the old lady who runs the mailroom came back from lunch early and almost caught me.

Q.   One mistake was all it took, pal. But I'm not interested in that. I'm investigating a murder. I promise I'll have more questions to ask you again, soon.

Bonny was typing up notes at her desk when Punch returned from lunch the next day. He stood behind her and casually brushed his fingers across the nape of her neck. She looked up startled, then blushed. Her eyes darted around the room to see if any of the other detectives had noticed the intimate gesture, but everyone appeared absorbed in their own work.

"Any luck?" Punch asked.

"You were right about R and I," Bonny said. "They had nothing on Johnson *or* Johanssen. So I went to the Motion Picture Academy library. They had twelve indexed volumes on the HUAC hearings in Los Angeles. Apparently, Eva's father was one of the first to testify. He named twelve people in the industry, two women and ten men, who he claimed were Communists. I'm typing up the list now."

"Any familiar names?"

"Only one. A Roger Millett. You remember that read-out I got from R and I on the mourners? Wasn't there a Millett on it?"

"Sounds familiar," said Punch. "I'll look it up."

Back in his office, Punch studied the Johnson homicide file, which was now a quarter of an inch thick. He found the original R and I report and Bud Millett's name.

"You were right," Punch told Bonny, looking up from the file. "It says here this Bud Millett was busted twice for possession, and he works as a film studio technician. Check the employment office at the studio and find out if he worked on any of Eva's pictures. Then check with my contact at TRW, the credit people." Punch looked through his card file and wrote a name and number on a piece of paper. "They'll have his current background and current address, and give us a good idea of his spending habits. I'll get Waite to run a background check on the other names."

"I've read the transcript of your second interview with Matt Shaw, and there's no doubt in my mind that he's our murderer," the Chief told Punch over the telephone. "I've scheduled a press conference for four this afternoon, and I want you there."

"Is the press conference necessary, sir?" Punch asked. "I'd prefer to keep the heat on my other suspects rather than let them think the case is solved."

"At the moment the coroner's office is getting all the headlines with their announcement that Eva Johnson was murdered. It's time the public was aware that we also have a police department in Los Angeles."

"I'm not so certain Shaw is our man," said Punch.

"You have a better suspect?"

"No, sir. I'll agree Shaw is the most logical, but—"

The Chief interrupted: "Shaw had motive, expertise and access. Do the other suspects match those criteria?"

"Not yet, sir, but I haven't had time to check them out. After all, the homicide investigation started only a few days ago."

"You don't have to remind me when it started, Captain." The Chief's voice was icy with sarcasm. "I am reminded of that every day by the press and the commission. And I don't think *I* need to remind *you* of our conversation concerning this case."

"No, sir, you don't."

"Then I'll expect to see you in my office at four P.M."

The Chief was especially in his glory when he could announce—as though he were personally responsible—a suspect or a solution to any one of the fifty or so homicides that occur weekly in Los Angeles, and the murder of Eva Johnson was one of the most publicized in recent history.

Punch stood alongside the Chief. His boss was dressed for the role in a subdued business suit. Microphones were lined up in front of him like toy soldiers. His office was bright as an operating room from the TV lights. A statement prepared by the public relations department was on the desk in front of him.

Promptly at four, the Chief coughed discreetly. The news people, to that moment jockeying for position, quickly settled down and quieted. The Chief sat erect in his chair, hands spread alongside the prepared statement. He paused and waited a moment to be certain he had everyone's attention.

"A suspect has been charged with the murder of producer Eva Johnson. The suspect will be indicted as soon as possible, and arraigned within the next few days."

"What's his name?" a female reporter asked.

"Must a murderer always be a man?" the Chief asked jocularly.

There were a few murmurs of laughter.

"But it happens that in this case, it *is* a man," the Chief continued. "At the moment, the individual is only a suspect, and to protect his rights, I must withhold his name until the formal indictment—which, as I said, will be very soon."

"How was she murdered?"

"With a most sophisticated device that required immense expertise. All I can tell you now is that it was a most fiendish device."

Well, he did it, Punch thought. He gave them their headline: "PRODUCER KILLED BY FIENDISH DEVICE."

"The investigation required the combined efforts of all the investigative and scientific branches of the police department, and was spearheaded by Captain Phillip Roberts of Robbery-Homicide." The Chief nodded toward Punch who self-consciously acknowledged the members of the press. "The investigation is still continuing to determine whether the suspect had accomplices."

During the brief question-and-answer period that followed, to which the Chief supplied noncommittal replies, Punch sat uncomfortably. The Chief was clearly convinced the evidence showed Matt was guilty, and that any D.A. would go along with it. There was only one problem. Circumstantial evidence to the contrary, Punch had a strong sense that Matt was not guilty. It was the kind of intuition, Punch thought with a shiver, that either made a detective's career or broke it. It could also make or break an innocent man's life.

Sally Shaffer was tired. Her last visitor had given her a pill from the medicine cabinet before leaving. It had been a long and straining visit but when it ended she felt at peace; an old wrong had finally been set right. She tucked the patchwork quilt around her frail body and settled back to doze. A sudden searing pain brought her erect, eyes wide with fear. She died trying to reach for the nurse's buzzer.

"How'd it go?" Bonny asked when Punch returned from the press conference.

"The Old Man made it sound as though the case was closed. How'd it go on your end?"

"Well, I discovered that Bud Millett was listed as an assistant director on *The Reckoning*." Bonny paused to let the information sink in. "And your friend at TRW told me Millett's credit rating was super-good. He pays his bills on time and in full. From the list of his purchases for the last year, though, he must have an independent income. He spent more than eighty thousand dollars during the last ten months."

Punch whistled softly. "That's too much money for someone with his job. He's either blackmailing someone or he's still pushing." Punch tugged lightly on his ear. "Tell you what, Sprout, you keep on checking Millett out: family history, the whole bit."

Punch turned to an inch-thick stack of paper lying on top of his "IN" basket, reports updating him on the progress of more than thirty cases his detectives were currently investigating. He reached into a pocket of the jacket draped over the back of his chair and removed a pair of reading glasses smudged with lint and fingerprints. Pulling a section of shirt from his pants, he blew on the glasses, and wiped them almost clean. He tucked the shirt back in, put the glasses on the tip of his nose, took a deep breath, and began to study the reports, making comments or suggestions on each one.

On a single page labeled "Investigation into the Attempted Shooting of Officer Cutler" he found a handwritten note from Detective Waite:

> Word on the street from my best informants is that Tony Hilpert, older brother of the man killed by Detective Bonny Cutler, has threatened revenge for his brother's death. Tony Hilpert was released on parole from San Quentin on January 18, 1981, after serving four years of a seven-year sentence for armed robbery.

Punch rocked back in his desk chair and smiled grimly. He looked out the window at the brightly lit New Otani. "That son of a bitch," he muttered. "It *was* Hilpert who tried to kill Bonny." Punch typed a memo to Communications instructing them to put out an APB on Hilpert.

It was after six when he finished his paperwork, and the night shift was coming in for duty. He had told Bonny he'd be home for dinner at eight. He started to light a cigarette when the telephone rang.

"Captain Roberts?"

"Speaking."

"This is Bertha Pasternack. I'm the administrator at

the Motion Picture Country Home, and a good friend of Sally Shaffer's. She spoke of you often and did nothing but talk about your visit with her earlier in the week."

"Is Sally all right?" Punch asked.

"She died this afternoon."

"Oh, my God, I'm sorry," Punch said. "How did it happen?"

"Her heart just gave out." The woman's voice broke. "Sally was old, you know, but she was in such high spirits. It's hard to believe."

"I'm truly sorry," Punch said. "When is the funeral?"

"Monday at two at Forest Lawn in Glendale. There's only Sally's son left, you know, and he asked me to make the funeral arrangements since I knew Sally and was her friend for so many years." Mrs. Pasternack paused and coughed discreetly. "I'm asking some friends of Sally's from the industry to eulogize her. I wonder if you'd mind saying a few words? Nothing formal. But a police captain"—Mrs Pasternack started to sob—"and she had so much respect for you . . . it would be nice to have someone not in show business. . . ."

"I'd be honored," Punch said.

Punch took off his glasses and looked out the window. Santa Ana winds were blowing in from the Southeast. As long as he had lived in Los Angeles, Punch had never liked the hot, dry winds. He believed they made people do evil things.

Something clicked in his mind. He reached for the telephone and dialed Bob Dahlstrom's office. Dahlstrom answered.

"Bob, I want you to do something for me."

"Anything you want, partner, but I hope it can wait until tomorrow. I was just closing up shop, and my old lady'll kill me if I'm late for supper."

"Sally Shaffer, the gossip columnist, just died at the Motion Picture Country Home in Woodland Hills. I'll get an order for the inquest. Can you arrange to have the body picked up and autopsied real quick? The funeral is Monday afternoon."

"What was the cause of death?"

"Her heart gave out."

"She must have been a very old lady, Punch. Chances are, the doctor at the home has already signed her death off as heart failure."

"I'm sure that's the way it reads, but that's also the way your man diagnosed Eva Johnson's death at first. Look, Bob, I know this is a long shot, but I'll take full responsibility for making it priority."

Dahlstrom sighed. "You handle the paperwork and I'll have the body picked up tonight. I'll do the P.M. myself first thing in the morning. Will that satisfy you?"

"I will, and thanks. Just one more thing. You know what to look for."

"I know what to look for."

After Dahlstrom hung up, Punch dialed the number of the Motion Picture Country Home. He asked for Mrs. Pasternack.

"This is Captain Roberts again. I wonder if you'd do a favor for me?"

"If I can."

"I'd like a list of Sally's visitors during the past week."

"I can do that," the woman said. "We keep a guest register."

"Good," said Punch. "I'll call you for it tomorrow morning."

"When are you coming to bed?" Bonny asked.

Punch was sitting in an old easy chair with Sally's scrapbook open on his lap.

"You go to bed, Sprout. I'll be along soon," he called over his shoulder.

"You've spent the whole evening reading that scrapbook. What are you looking for?"

Punch tugged at his ear. "I'm not sure, but I'll know it if I find it. Anyway, just reading her old columns has given me some ideas of what I might say Monday."

Bonny came over and kissed him on the cheek. "I'm going to watch TV for a while."

"Okay, hon. I'll be along soon."

Nearly two hours later, Punch thumped the scrapbook closed. When he came into the bedroom, Bonny was still awake. "Did you find anything interesting?" she asked.

"I did."

"Want to tell me about it?"

"Later. I still have a couple of loose ends to sort out. But some things are beginning to fall into place."

CHAPTER *13*

Punch studied the list of Sally's recent visitors who had been notified of the funeral. Quite impressive. The list included Reese Donovan, Evan Sadler, David Braverman and Mickey Levy.

"I didn't know Sally was a friend of Mickey Levy's," he said to Mrs. Pasternack over the telephone.

The administrator for the Motion Picture Country Home laughed lightly. "Sally had friends in all walks of life. You know, back in the forties and fifties Mickey was the most notorious gangster on the West Coast. That made him a celebrity. And celebrities were Sally's business. When Sally came to live here, Levy sent her a dozen roses every week. He visited often and talked about old times."

"Did Reese Donovan visit Sally alone, or was his wife with him?"

"He was alone. I know because he had been one of my favorite stars for years. When I heard he was visiting Sally, I would drop in, too. He was just as charming in person as on the screen. He even gave me an autograph."

Punch glanced at the list again. Three of his suspects had visited Sally, plus one other person whose name he underlined twice. "Have you notified all of Sally's friends about the funeral?"

"All those I could reach," said Mrs. Pasternack.

"Including the people on the list you just read to me?"

"Yes, and they all said they'd be there. Oh, there will also be notices in the trade papers tomorrow listing the time and place."

"Good," said Punch. "One more thing. Can you arrange it so I am the last one to speak at the service?"

"If that's what you want."

Partial transcript of the third taped interrogation between Captain Phillip Roberts and Matt Shaw at Parker Center, Los Angeles, April 19, 1981, approximately 11:00 A.M.

Q: The last time we talked you thought of someone or something you didn't want to discuss. When we talked about bombs and then drugs, you said, and I quote, "Oh, my God." Do you remember that conversation?

A: I do.

Q: Do you know Bud Millett?

A: Yes.

Q: How well?

A: He worked on *The Reckoning.*

Q: What was his job?

A: He was a gofer, but I think they called him an assistant director.

Q: What's a gofer?

A: You know, a person who goes for things: coffee, cigarettes, anything that someone wants. Sometimes he helped the director.

Q: Did he have any other jobs?

A: None that I know of.

Q: Were there any other gofers on the set?

A: Not that I know of.

Q: Was he also pushing drugs?

A: Maybe. I don't know for sure.

Q: Stop bullshitting me, Shaw. We both know what
     Millett was doing, so why are you covering for him?
     Were you a pusher, too?

A: No. I guess maybe he was pushing, but I never saw a
     buy go down.

Q: Did Eva use drugs occasionally?

A: Yeah, I told you already. But she was no addict.

Q: This Millett, was he her pusher?

A: I guess when she had drugs, she probably got them
     from him.

Q: Is that why he was hired? I mean, does every set
     have a pusher to keep everyone happy?

A: I don't know anything about other sets. And I don't
     know why he was hired. I asked Eva about him once
     and she said she owed him a big one.

Q: Is he the person you thought of and wouldn't discuss?

A: Yes.

Q: Why were you covering for him?

A: I didn't want to get anyone else in trouble.

Q: You don't seem to realize, you're the one who's in
     trouble, big trouble.

Punch called Dahlstrom as soon as he finished with
Matt. An operator said the deputy coroner was probably in
the lab.

"Switch me over, please," Punch said.

Dahlstrom came on the line.

"You must be clairvoyant or a gypsy genius,"
Dahlstrom said. "The mortuary just picked up Sally
Shaffer's body for the funeral and, Punch, you were right!
The cause of death was perforation of the lung and aorta—
by a minute explosion. I can't make it a hundred percent
until we run more tests, but the similarity between her
death and the Johnson girl's is there. Also I found the same
kind of foreign matter in Sally's vital organs as we found in
Eva Johnson."

"Thanks, Bob."

". . . And I want you all dressed like mourners," Punch told the five detectives gathered in front of his desk. You're to mingle until I start the eulogy."

He pointed to a black and white photo on his desk. "Take one last look at that face. I don't want any slip-ups."

He studied the detectives. "Any questions? No? All right, then. You've got your assignments." And I have mine, he thought.

Punch handed an official form to Detective Waite. "Here's the search warrant," he said, "but try and get in when the house is empty."

CHAPTER *14*

Punch had been to Forest Lawn often in recent years. Each time he drove onto the cemetery grounds he got depressed, made aware not only of the passing of time and the loss of friends, but of his own mortality.

He and Bonny were in a line of cars moving slowly up Cathedral Drive. Bonny was wearing a navy blue suit and clutching a blue leather purse on her lap. The winds had died down and now it was still and stiflingly hot. Punch, wearing his dark blue suit, was conscious from the snugness of the shirt collar that he had gained weight. If the cigarettes haven't killed me, I'll die of a heart attack, he thought, because now I'm overweight from having given up smoking.

"Goddamn county," he said aloud. "You'd think they'd let us have air conditioning in these cars." It was a complaint he registered regularly on a hot day.

"It's for economy," Bonny said. "You've told me yourself, air conditioning eats up gas."

The line of cars was now crawling up Inspiration Slope. Gardeners were weeding the carpet of luxuriant green

166

grass that covered all the landscape in sight. Headstones set flush with the ground were barely visible from the road.

"It's a shame you never knew Sally," Punch said as the cortege slowed to a halt. "She was a salty old character, a real pistol when she was Queen Bee in Hollywood. Which is why I liked her."

"If all these people are going to her funeral, I'd say she had a lot of friends," Bonny said.

"They were afraid to cross her when she was alive, and they're probably still afraid of her. Most likely they're afraid to miss her funeral."

The procession began to move forward again, and then stopped. Now they could see that the cause of the delay was an elderly man wearing black pants and a green coat, with a white sea captain's cap perched incongruously on his head. He was stopping each car.

"Shaffer services?" he asked Punch.

"Yes."

"Park to your right in the circular driveway ahead." The old man had a mellifluous voice.

"Sounds like he's out of Central Casting," Bonny said as they parked and locked the car.

"He's on the wrong set," Punch said. "He belongs in a sea epic."

They fell in line with a stream of other arrivals.

"Ahead of us, look," Bonny whispered excitedly.

"Where?" Punch was instantly alert.

"There's Charlton Heston!"

"Damn it, Sprout, we're not tourists." Punch's voice was heavy with exasperation, but he, too, looked at the tall, handsome actor with interest. Punch recognized other celebrities, but his eyes were searching for his four other detectives in the crowd gathered on the fieldstone walkway, waiting their turn to enter the Church of the Recessional, a replica of an old English church with narrow, stained-glass windows and a slate roof.

He caught sight of Detectives Waite and Bernheim

standing together among a group of mourners by the entrance. Punch realized it was the first time he had ever seen them dressed up. The other two detectives were probably already inside. Waite attracted Punch's attention and nodded affirmatively: the person had already entered.

The interior of the church was cool, the floor carpeted in soft mauve pile. "I'm surprised the pews aren't upholstered," Punch whispered to Bonny as they crowded together on the oak bench at the end of an aisle.

On the dais, elevated by two steps from the seating area, was a closed coffin covered with white gardenias. To its right was an oak-covered lattice, obscuring an area reserved for the family. The sound of sobbing came from behind the lattice. Punch felt sad that he knew nothing of Sally's family except for his brief encounter with her late husband and Sally's occasional mention of a son.

Glancing around the group gathered to pay their last respects, Punch was pleased to see the church so crowded. He remembered how proud he had been at the number of people who came to pay homage to his father.

A young man in a charcoal business suit stepped onto the dais, and the crowd hushed. Referring to notes, he said, "It was Sally's request that there be no formal services at this time. Sally always decried formality, and disliked what she termed the hypocrisy of eulogies. It was her wish that those of her friends who had something to say about her, good or bad, be permitted to speak. 'They can roast or toast me,' she said. 'It'll be their last chance.'"

There were appreciative murmurs from the audience. An elderly woman in a print dress and a blue straw hat joined him on the dais. Turning to her he said, "Mrs. Bertha Pasternack, the administrator from the Motion Picture Country Home, has been in contact with some of Sally's friends who expressed a desire to say a few words."

Punch listened to the various speakers with only half an ear. He was keeping his eye on his suspects—many of whom had gathered here—and on his four detectives. Waite and Bernheim were seated on the aisles of the last pews at the rear of the church. The other two were seated directly behind the person whose photo he had given them at yesterday's briefing. The stage was set.

Mrs. Pasternack called his name and Bonny nudged him gently in the ribs. Punch walked slowly to the dais. He had been so busy with his thoughts until that moment that he had no time for stage fright. Now, confronted by so many celebrities under such solemn circumstances, he began to have second thoughts about what he planned to say.

He cleared his throat and started to speak. "Mrs. Pasternack introduced me by name, but she neglected to give my profession. I am a captain of Robbery-Homicide for the Los Angeles Police Department. Today I am here in two capacities: as a longtime friend and admirer of Sally's, and as a law-enforcement officer."

His introduction had the desired effect. He had everyone's attention.

"I met Sally under unusual circumstances some twenty years ago," he continued. "I had the occasion to help her husband, and she and I became good friends. She was, as you all know, a mine of information about the people in her town. She was always available to me for wise counsel or helpful suggestions when I contacted her about a case. She earned her reputation as a gossip columnist, but she never gossiped with me or revealed information she had learned in confidence. She dealt only with facts, and I respected her for that.

"I had the good fortune to visit Sally during the last few days of her life, and she was spunky and irascible as ever."

A few people laughed.

"She was as concerned about me and my life as I was about hers, which was typical of her. I had gone to see her because I needed help with a homicide I was investigating—the murder of Eva Johnson at the Academy Awards ceremony two weeks ago.

"Like most newspaper people, Sally was fascinated

with police work. She was an experienced reporter, and understood the process: investigation of facts, following up leads, interviews, and the like. At our last visit I asked Sally to brief me on a period of local history which many of you recall and the rest of you have probably heard about—that black time in the early fifties when the House Un-American Activities Committee was investigating communism in Hollywood. Sally hated communism and what she believed it stood for. She took the popular position that Communists should be rooted out of America and, in particular, out of her beloved film industry. As a patriot, she felt it her duty to keep her readers informed of the committee's investigation into Hollywood. In her efforts to do good, however, she unintentionally harmed a few innocent people."

Punch was aware that some people in the congregation were beginning to shift restlessly in the pews. His eyes focused on the person sitting with an impassive face just in front of his detectives.

"I know that some of you are wondering what point I am going to make at this time, when we are all gathered to pay final tribute and homage to a woman we loved and will miss. But if you will bear with me for just a few more minutes, you will see. I know that Sally would be sitting on the edge of her seat by now, because she always loved a mystery—and this one would have special appeal to her."

Punch paused. The rustling had stopped. "The elements of this homicide investigation included sex and violence."

Reese and Cheryl Donovan shifted uncomfortably in their seats.

"Blackmail." Beads of sweat began to form on Mickey Levy's forehead. "Studio politics." David Braverman dropped his eyes. "Fraud." Evan Sadler's face paled. "And not one, but *three* murders."

There was a slight murmur of confusion from the mourners.

"The story began when Eva Johnson's father, Jack

Johanssen, a film producer, became one of the first to testify before the House Un-American Activities Committee in Washington on alleged Communist infiltration in Hollywood. The Fifth Amendment had not been invoked yet as a matter of form, and on the advice of his lawyer, Bernie Gruzinsky, Johanssen named some of his friends and co-workers. Although his testimony was given in closed hearings"– Punch turned slightly toward the coffin–"it was leaked to Sally, who printed his accusations and the names of those he accused.

"I know for a fact that Sally, here, regretted, even up to a few days ago, her failure to check some facts as thoroughly as she might have. She told me she hadn't realized that, working in the industry at that time, were *two* men who had the same first and last name. Although one of them later admitted he was a Communist and quit the business, the other denied the charges. But he was nevertheless blacklisted, forced out of his livelihood as a film director, had to take menial jobs to survive. Sally tried to set the record straight with a retraction. But it was too late–the damage had been done. This unjustly accused man became so distraught he committed suicide, leaving behind a son about the same age as Eva Johnson.

"That young man grew up with a cloud of social disgrace over his head. Because of Sally's error, the film community believed that his father had been a Communist conspirator, a traitor to his country. Eva grew up in pain, too. Her father was an informer. The family changed its name to Johnson and sent Eva away to school in the East. The young man went into the Army, where he later distinguished himself with two Bronze Stars in Vietnam."

Punch slowly scanned the first few rows of the chapel. His delivery softened, slowed, and became more deliberate. "He also became a user of drugs, a habit he continued after his discharge and return to Hollywood. Meanwhile, Eva finished college and returned to Los Angeles to start work at a film studio. There she met Elliott Gruzinsky, a young writer. They had a common bond. His father had been her father's lawyer in the HUAC hearings, the man who advised Jack Johanssen to name names. She bought a script from Elliott and produced it as her first film."

Punch paused again, taking in the confusion on the faces before him. He only hoped he knew where he was leading them.

"At about this time, Eva became aware of the son of the innocent man who had suffered because of her father's testimony and Sally's columns. Out of compassion for him— or perhaps guilt—she gave him a low-level job on her film. He was soon to find a niche, however. He became the film company drug pusher."

The person sitting in front of his detectives returned Punch's gaze defiantly.

"I can only speculate on this young man's earlier state of mind. Here he was working with two descendants of the people he must have felt were responsible for his father's death. He must have hated them very much, and resented their success. And he must have hated Sally, who had published the story that destroyed his father."

Punch suddenly stopped. Millett was holding a black box about the size of a pack of cigarettes. He looked at Punch with a triumphant smile as his finger slowly nudged up a tiny antenna. The one thing Punch hadn't foreseen. He had a knot in his throat.

The congregation craned in unison to see who Punch was looking at. Millett stood up. So did the detectives behind him. Punch motioned for them to remain still.

"A good speech, Captain," said Millett. "But not complete."

Everyone turned toward Millett, who moved out of the pew into the center aisle and headed toward Punch, clutching the black box in front of him like a shield. Punch signaled that his two detectives should remain in their seats.

"Did I leave something out, Mr. Millett?" Punch asked quietly.

"These people here, all of them, they should remember my father, Roger Millett, and what they did to him. Do you know why that good man, that *innocent* man, committed suicide? Because of that evil woman in the coffin behind you. Because of her mistake! She ran a retraction, all right, but it was too late. Even after he was cleared, the stigma remained. No one, not even his friends, would hire him again. This goddamned town and its goddamned spineless people!"

Millett looked around at the congregation. "Most of you were part of the Hollywood scene then. You all knew my father. Many of you had worked with him. He was a brilliant director! But when he died, six people showed up at his funeral. *Six people!* And you all came here to pay your respects to the woman who helped destroy him. You bastards!"

The crowd murmured angrily.

Punch held up his hands. "Easy," he said, "the man has a point he wants to make. This may not be the proper time or place, but let him have his say."

"Very wise, Captain," said Millett, "but you're not interested in my point. You're interested in what I'm holding in my hand." He showed the black box to the congregation. "Let me interest you a little further. The moment there's an absence of pressure on this plunger I'm holding down with my thumb, the roof's going to come tumbling down."

Millett laughed crazily and turned around to face the group, holding the black box aloft. "My very own doomsday machine," he announced.

A couple at the rear of the chapel broke for the door.

"Don't anyone leave or everyone dies!" Millett screamed.

The couple froze. Terrified, they returned to their seats. Punch used the distraction to signal Waite and Bernheim, pointing his thumb toward the roof.

"I don't understand you, Millett," Punch said, stalling for time. "Why now, why after thirty years?"

"Because people are writing books about how *everyone*

was a victim in those days. Well, I don't buy that. Sally Shaffer was no victim. And I can't feel sorry for old man Johanssen or his lawyer, Gruzinsky. *They* were the enemy, *they* had a choice. I can't help it if they made the wrong one. But my father was innocent! He never had a choice! He never had a trial! He was innocent! This fucking town found him guilty. He *was* a victim, and he was innocent."

An elderly man sitting near Millett got angrily to his feet. "Damn you, get out or I'll throw you out," he said, approaching Millett threateningly.

In the confusion, Punch saw Waite, Bernheim and Bonny slip out the front door.

"Tell this old fool, Captain," Millett said gleefully. "Tell him what I have in my hands, or shall I give it to him?"

"He's holding a detonator," Punch said. "He probably has explosives hidden somewhere. Don't go near him."

There was a concerted gasp of horror from the audience. A woman screamed, some started to sob.

"Settle down," Punch ordered. "We're all hostages until this young man gets what he wants. Let's listen to him. Panic will be counterproductive."

Waite was the first detective out of the church. He waited for the others to join him outside. The wall of the building was solid flagstone, he noted, with a rain gutter running underneath the projecting overhang about seven feet off the ground.

"We'll boost you first because you're the lightest," Waite told Bonny as all three removed their shoes. "I'll help Bernie and he'll pull me up. We'll take the gutters. You search the vents, bell tower, and chimney."

The two detectives made a step of their hands for Bonny.

"What am I looking for?" she whispered as she clambered onto the roof.

"That's a good question," Waite replied.

"Please! Don't anybody move," Punch ordered. "Maybe we can convince this young man to see reason."

The congregation was getting edgy. Facing Millett, he said, "Don't you realize you're doing the same thing to these people that you say Hollywood did to your father? You're going to destroy innocent people without a trial, without cause. Do you want to go down in history as a mass murderer *and* a suicide? Because that's how you'll be remembered, not as a hero who avenged his father's wrongful death."

"These aren't people, they're animals!" yelled Millett. "They wouldn't know a fair trial if they saw one. And 'without cause'! You must be kidding!" He laughed hysterically. "*You,*" Millett said, pointing to an elderly man on an aisle seat, "Mike Stuart, you held me on your lap when I was a kid, but when my father couldn't get any work and needed you as a friend, then where were you?" He whirled around. "Beverly Homack, my father made you a star, but when he needed you for leverage to get a new picture going, you didn't return his calls. Morris Koenig, after my father had directed half a dozen successful movies for you, *you* wouldn't hire him." Millett was nearly shrieking now. "I know who you all are, and you're no better today than you were then. You all stink with your 'virtue.' But the world should know how corrupt you really are. And when we all hit the six o'clock news, everyone will!"

Bonny struggled to maintain her purchase on the slippery slate tiles. It wasn't easy in stockinged feet. Moving carefully to make a minimum of noise, she peered inside each air vent, then put her hand in as far as she could reach, feeling for anything that seemed odd.

She crept over to the bell tower. Grateful to have something to get a firm grip on, she straightened up and examined the bell, then the clapper, and found nothing. She ran her hands along the inside of the jagged brick structure. Nothing.

"You say you want to make public the crimes against your father?" Directly below her she could hear Punch's voice filtering up.

Punch stalled for time, trying to keep Millett's attention focused on him. "You know who's going to jail for at least one of those deaths, don't you? Your friend Matt Shaw."

Millett's eyes narrowed.

"Sure he will," said Punch. "He murdered Eva Johnson. He had motive. And he had access, too, didn't he? We don't know exactly how he did it yet, but at the moment, he's number one. Just a jilted lover's revenge."

"No," Millett's voice was quiet and certain.

"Of course it was," said Punch, "and we have our lab guys working on it right now to figure out just how Matt did it."

Bud pursed his lips and took a deep breath. "I can save you the trouble."

"You can? How?"

"Matt didn't do it. I did."

"Look, Millett, you're probably very upset, and you don't realize what you've just said. Now, why don't we all just forget we heard you."

"Goddamn you, Matt didn't do it. He sure had reason to, but he didn't. I did." His jaw jutted forward. "I'll even tell you how."

"Sure, anything to protect your friend."

"All right, smartass, listen to this." Millett's eyes darted around. Punch concentrated intently on Millett's finger, which still depressed the trigger mechanism on the transmitter.

"Eva asked me to come out to her place early Monday afternoon with some pills that would relax her before the Awards ceremony," Millett said. "She didn't know Matt had told me he'd helped fix it so she would win."

Several people looked in Evan Sadler's direction, their

eyes reflecting astonishment at Millett's revelation. Sadler's face turned ashen and he shrank in his seat.

"When I learned Eva had dumped Matt, I felt sorry for him—you see, he hadn't grown up in Hollywood, he didn't understand how you people do things. Eva Johnson was completely amoral. Her father's daughter in every way. Without losing so much as a night's sleep, she arranged events to suit herself. But what the hell! She wasn't so unusual, was she?" he asked the crowd. "This whole room is full of Eva Johnsons. But the score always evens up for *everyone*," he said, looking slowly around him. "I wasn't going to let her get away with it.

"The pill I gave her that Monday was one I'd made up myself. You know that theme from her movie with that high trumpet note at the climax? The 'pill' was programmed to go off with that last high note. I'd recorded it at the run-through rehearsal. When the orchestra hit that note—bang! It was perfect!"

Millett's eyes were gleaming, his voice triumphant. Punch wanted to keep him talking.

"But," Punch said, "she gave you a job on her film."

"A job, hah, that's a laugh. She hired me as a gofer to ease her conscience. Then she found out I could be useful because I had heavy contacts in drugs. She used me, too, turned me into a pusher for her and her friends—like Gruzinsky."

"What had *he* done to you?" Punch asked, calculating his chances of rushing Millett and squeezing the boy's hand on the lever. He decided against it. A split second late and they'd all be blood and dust. He hoped his people were already on the roof.

"Gruzinsky was no better than Eva," Bud said. "He and Eva were friends when I met him. After he had a falling out with Eva, we stayed in touch. He had a gram-a-day habit, and I kept him going. Last time I saw him, I made a delivery of coke, and stuck a bomb under his workbench, timed to go off half an hour after I left. I knew he wouldn't wait long to start with the free-base—and he didn't. Pow! Perfect!"

"What about Sally?" Punch asked quietly.

Until that moment, the dazed audience had been observing the exchange between Punch and Millett as though they were watching a play or a drama unfolding on television. Only a few of them had known Eva personally. Less than a handful had been aware of Gruzinsky's existence, let alone his death. But they had all known Sally. Suddenly they were no longer detached. There were murmurs of shock and horror.

"I went to visit her two days ago to tell her I'd heard she was sick. I didn't want her to die feeling guilty for my father's suicide." Millett laughed again. "That's what I told her, and she actually *thanked* me. She said he'd been on her conscience. I knew if she was sick she'd be taking lots of pills, so I brought an assortment of mine with me, planning to slip her one. Then before I left"—his voice took on a sly tone—"she asked me to give her a pill from her medicine cabinet. Half an hour later, from the parking lot, I punched the button on my transmitter. Pow! Three!"

"But why do you feel that all of us here deserve to die?"

"I've already told you, because all of you were part of the conspiracy to kill my father. You were all part of the Establishment then, you still are. You're all corrupt! You've never helped anyone but yourselves. You've put your feet in the faces of everyone on the ladder below you."

"What will you achieve by killing us?" Punch realized Millett's patience was running out, but each question bought more time.

One of the tiles under Bonny's foot loosened and slipped a few inches, throwing her off balance. She grabbed the ledge of the bell tower.

Inside the chapel, the sound expanded and echoed. Everyone's head snapped up toward the roof. "Shit!"

thought Punch, as he moved from behind the podium, ready to leap onto Millett.

Bonny's fingers had touched a small package taped under the ledge of the tower. She pulled it off and held it up for Waite and Bernheim to see.

"So, you got somebody up there," Millett yelled. "We got something better down here. You'll need this for evidence, too!" He held up the transmitter.

Bernheim gestured wildly for Bonny to throw the package. She fumbled. The package fell from her hand and slid down the tiled incline just past Waite, who dove to the ground after it.

Millett lifted his finger.

"It was like an earthquake. The walls shook. The stained-glass windows shattered. People were screaming—"

Bernheim interrupted Punch. "My ears are still ringing from the concussion. It knocked us all flat. Luckily Waite threw the bomb into a grove of trees, which absorbed most of the explosion."

The Chief, grim-faced, listened to Punch and his five detectives stonily. "You placed the lives of more than two hundred people in jeopardy. Explain yourself!"

"I misjudged how dangerous Millett was," Punch admitted. "I knew he was guilty of three murders, but when Waite and Bernheim made a search of the premises, they only came up with a mold for making pills. He must have manufactured the explosive contents and the detonators elsewhere. All I had to go on was a hunch and some circumstantial evidence, barely enough to bring him in for questioning.

"Then I found out he was one of Sally's last visitors, and had been invited to the funeral. When I was asked to deliver a eulogy, I figured it was the perfect opportunity to put public pressure on him—since he was obviously unbalanced—maybe provoke him into a careless remark or move of some kind that would be an admission of guilt, if not a confession."

"You endangered all those lives to test a notion?" The Chief's voice was heavy with sarcasm.

"I underestimated the man," Punch said. "I knew his motive for wanting to kill Eva, Gruzinsky, and Sally—but I had no idea he would try to wipe out the rest of Hollywood! So I took a chance, ordered five detectives to pose as mourners, and planned what I would say in my eulogy. I thought I had covered all the bases."

Bonny spoke up. "If we hadn't been there, Chief, the bomb would have gone off and most of those people would have been killed or injured."

The Chief drummed his fingers on the desk blotter. "What you're telling me is that Captain Roberts ought to be congratulated for saving those lives instead of risking them."

"No, sir," said Punch heatedly. "What I'm saying is that I acted out of the best evidence I had, but that I didn't know just how crazy Millett was. Thank God no one was hurt, and we collared him."

"Why were you so certain Shaw wasn't the killer?" the Chief asked.

"He *was* the logical suspect for Eva's murder since he knew explosives and had been rejected by her, but there was no reason at all for him to kill Gruzinsky, and he was in custody when Sally died."

The Chief considered Punch's answer for a moment. For the first time he relaxed and smiled. "All right, Captain. Now why don't you all sit down while Captain Roberts fills me in on what I am to tell the press."

The men sat down. Punch drew up a chair for Bonny. The Chief acknowledged the gesture with a wry smile.

"At first, Chief, everyone had a motive; Gruzinsky, Braverman, Eva's ex-husband, Nicholas Riddle, Levy, Donovan. There was even something odd about the mother's story and her relationship with the stockbroker, Nelson. My guess is they were having an affair and she tried to hock Eva's jewelry to cover up a bad investment she had made with her daughter's money. Then we found most of them had been at the Awards ceremony, which was easily checked. They all had an alibi at the moment of Eva's death.

"It was Coroner Dahlstrom who knocked all the alibis into a cocked hat when he discovered Eva had been killed by a mini-bomb that she swallowed. He put me onto the boys in the bomb squad, who identified the explosive as an azide, which was used in 'Nam. Dahlstrom put me on to a government expert who said the bomb could be triggered by an impulse, possibly from a transmitter, maybe a laser beam, or even activated by a special sound. I knew then we were dealing with someone familiar with leading-edge technology. But that also meant none of the alibis stood up. Anyone, anywhere, could have detonated that device.

"Then Gruzinsky was killed by an explosion and his death was made to look like an accident. I might have bought that story, except Dahlstrom found traces of azide in what was left of his body.

"From there on it was primarily a question of discovering what the three victims had in common. Detective Cutler suggested the clue to Eva's death might be in her childhood or family history, which led me to Mrs. Johnson, who revealed the relationship between Eva and Gruzinsky. Sally Shaffer had lent me her scrapbook, and I found that she had identified Millett's father as a Communist, then later retracted it. But that tied Sally in with the others.

"R and I provided the missing link: Millett had worked on *The Reckoning*, which meant he knew Eva and Gruzinsky. And Gruzinsky had developed the original script, and was around until Eva fired him. After Sally was killed in the same manner as Eva, Shaw told me about Millett's background in 'Nam. And, as you know, we got a warrant to search Millett's premises.

"Detectives Waite and Bernheim learned from Millett's neighbors that pets and wild animals in the neighborhood had been dying mysteriously and suddenly, which meant he was probably experimenting with his bombs. You know the rest. Millett has confessed."

"What have you done about Shaw?" the Chief asked.

"I asked the D.A. to order his release. He's probably on the street by now."

"Has the Fraud Squad been informed about his role in the Awards?"

"Not by me," said Punch. "It's up to Sadler's organization to press charges."

The Chief glanced at his watch and stood up. "If you'll all excuse me, I have a press conference in twenty minutes."

The five detectives saluted. He looked at Waite and Bernheim. "There will be commendations added to your files for your roles in this case. Now I want a word alone with Captain Roberts and Detective Cutler."

After the door closed behind the men, the Chief walked around to Punch and Bonny. He offered Punch his hand. "Well done, Captain," he said. "Unorthodox procedure, but all's well that ends well. Trite, but in this instance, true. And my congratulations to you, too, Detective Cutler."

"Thank you, sir," Bonny said.

The Chief escorted them to the door. "When are you going to make it legal?" he asked with a wink. "Do us all a favor and don't let me hear anything else about you two but the date."